Three armed [men] the head of [...]

They were debating something that was also holding them back from approaching the office. The Executioner figured they had found the dead guy downstairs.

To Bolan's right was the door that led to the parking garage—it was the only way open to his escape.

Aware the three men might push caution ~~behind~~ them and head for the office, Bolan acted. He eased the door wide enough to let him through, raised the Beretta and powered into the corridor. He fired off two 3-round bursts in the general direction of the group and heard the startled shouts. Return shots, fired in haste, gouged the wall, sending plaster dust across the corridor. Bolan kept moving, committed to his action. He reached the door and shouldered it open. A final shot from his pursuers thudded into the door frame inches from Bolan's head. He slammed the door shut, knowing his freedom would be extremely short lived.

The thunder of boots approaching the door and the voices shouting back and forth warned him his time was running out fast. They had his scent. The hounds had taken up the chase and Bolan was the prize. The only thing they should have taken notice of was this prize had the choice of fighting back.

MACK BOLAN ®
The Executioner

The Executioner
Don Pendleton's
DEADLY COMMAND

A GOLD EAGLE BOOK FROM
WORLDWIDE®

TORONTO • NEW YORK • LONDON
AMSTERDAM • PARIS • SYDNEY • HAMBURG
STOCKHOLM • ATHENS • TOKYO • MILAN
MADRID • WARSAW • BUDAPEST • AUCKLAND

Recycling programs
for this product may
not exist in your area.

First edition April 2011

ISBN-13: 978-0-373-64389-9

Special thanks and acknowledgment to
Mike Linaker for his contribution to this work.

DEADLY COMMAND

Printed in U.S.A.

The art of war is simple enough. Find out where your enemy is. Get at him as soon as you can. Strike him as hard as you can and as often as you can, and keep moving on.

—Ulysses S. Grant
1822–1885

Those who supply the guns that kill innocent citizens can no longer keep their hands clean. I will hunt them down and end their game—hit them where it hurts, and hit them fast.

—Mack Bolan

THE
MACK BOLAN
LEGEND

Nothing less than a war could have fashioned the destiny of the man called Mack Bolan. Bolan earned the Executioner title in the jungle hell of Vietnam.

But this soldier also wore another name—Sergeant Mercy. He was so tagged because of the compassion he showed to wounded comrades-in-arms and Vietnamese civilians.

Mack Bolan's second tour of duty ended prematurely when he was given emergency leave to return home and bury his family, victims of the Mob. Then he declared a one-man war against the Mafia.

He confronted the Families head-on from coast to coast, and soon a hope of victory began to appear. But Bolan had broken society's every rule. That same society started gunning for this elusive warrior—to no avail.

So Bolan was offered amnesty to work within the system against terrorism. This time, as an employee of Uncle Sam, Bolan became Colonel John Phoenix. With a command center at Stony Man Farm in Virginia, he and his new allies—Able Team and Phoenix Force—waged relentless war on a new adversary: the KGB.

But when his one true love, April Rose, died at the hands of the Soviet terror machine, Bolan severed all ties with Establishment authority.

Now, after a lengthy lone-wolf struggle and much soul-searching, the Executioner has agreed to enter an "arm's-length" alliance with his government once more, reserving the right to pursue personal missions in his Everlasting War.

1

Miami, Florida

The background intel that set Mack Bolan, aka the Executioner, on his current mission had been encapsulated in frustration and not without a little impotent rage. Bolan had sensed the futility of the feelings behind the words transmitted via the interview that followed the triple funeral of slain police officers. He might not have even caught the televised segment if he had not been taking some downtime, following the completion of a mission he had undertaken at the behest of Hal Brognola, director of the Sensitive Operations Group, based at Stony Man Farm in Virginia. Bolan's chosen R & R had him chilling out in an expensive hotel on Florida's sunshine coast. It wasn't usual for Bolan to indulge in such opulent surroundings but his state of mind had allowed him a few days of rest, something he needed at that precise moment in time. After three days of allowing himself to relax, Bolan knew his downtime was not going to last for much longer and when he turned on that evening's newscast, the soldier realized just how true that was.

In a standoff with warring street gangs in Miami, five police officers had been fired on—three were dead, one was in a coma and the fifth still in critical condition. Two civilians caught in the cross fire were also dead. Eyewitness accounts had been corroborated in their descriptions of the weaponry used by the gangs. They had been using sophisticated arms, autorifles and the kind of ordnance not usually seen on the streets. A recovered weapon was shown. It was military ordnance, not available to the general public, and not even in use by the police.

The reporter, speaking to a Miami-Dade police officer, questioned why such weapons were on the streets. The cop, barely able to express himself calmly, said that the weapons were being supplied by organized crime groups, and that this was not the first time it had happened. The police had their suspicions as to who was behind the supply chain but had been unable to pursue any clear lines of evidence due to lack of solid proof.

The interview ended with a short piece on the funeral gathering, including shots of the four-year-old daughter of one of the slain officers placing a single rose on her father's casket. The look of bewilderment and the shine of tears on the girl's face caught Bolan off guard and he could relate to the held-back anger in the manner and tone of the cop who had been interviewed.

Bolan knew the man. He had worked with him on a mission that had taken the Executioner from Miami to an island off the Cuban mainland.

Gary Loomis was a good cop, a dedicated officer with the Miami-Dade force. Bolan remembered him clearly, and seeing the man's barely checked grief over the slain officers reminded the soldier of the daily risks police officers took when they placed themselves in the line of fire.

Later that night Bolan found himself recalling the young daughter of one of the dead police officers placing that single rose on her father's casket. It drifted back to him as he slept. It had been a long time since the soldier had been revisited by a disturbing vision—but the image of the child plagued him until he woke the following morning.

He called MDPD and was connected to Gary Loomis.

"Cooper? Hell, of course, I remember you." Loomis chuckled. "No way I'm liable to forget. So what can I do for you?"

"It's what I might be able to do for you, Loomis. Can we meet?"

"Sure. Give me an hour."

Bolan told the intrigued police officer where he was staying, then went down to have breakfast.

On the terrace they faced each other across a small table, having a drink. The Executioner and the Miami cop, men who walked through the shadow world of violence and corruption, one on the side of the law, the other who worked outside that law.

"I saw the interview," Bolan said.

"Bad time for Miami-Dade."

"You know those men personally?"

"Every damn one of them. Worked with them. Drank with them off duty. Knew their families, too."

"The girl who placed the rose?"

"Emily Crockett." Loomis stared into empty space for a moment, then cleared his throat. "Sweet kid. She'll be watched over. We take care of our own. Cooper, our guys never had a chance. They were cut down by state-of-the-art hardware. When I did some checking, I found out similar ordnance has turned up across the country. A definite in Chicago and Newark. I dig deeper. There's a pattern here. Too much weaponry being sent out. It's like a preamble for something bigger. The cops on the streets are our only line of defense against these bastards. Hell, Cooper, it's out of control and we can't keep up."

"Any link to the vendors?"

"The suppliers?" Loomis gripped his beer bottle until his knuckles turned white. "We have files on them, but nothing strong enough to give us just cause. No *real* evidence. Oh, we have a couple of local dirtbags we figure are the organization's crew, but we can't touch them without airtight proof, and we don't have that yet. They have lawyers on standby. They'd be back on the street before the charge sheets had finished printing. So we do nothing because if we screw up any investigation, that's it."

"So you have names? Locations?"

"Well, yeah. But what good…" Loomis stared at Bolan. "What the hell are you thinking, Cooper?"

Bolan raised his beer. "What *am* I thinking, Gary?"

Loomis gathered his thoughts before he spoke. "I know the way you operate, and your rules are way off-the-wall."

"We got results last time."

"Yeah, I know…but the department would go ape shit if we got involved in something illegal."

"The department isn't going to be involved. Or you. All I need are names and a place to start. After that you forget about me."

Loomis ran his hand across his face, taking a deep breath as he considered.

"Gary, if I'm compromising you, just walk away. I'll figure another way in."

"You could be dealing your way into something heavy. So don't be fooled into thinking they'll be easy marks."

"No chance of that."

Loomis stood up. "Be at the cemetery at five-thirty. Take a look at Jimmy Crockett's headstone. I'll be there, too."

"Yeah."

Before he moved Loomis said, "There has to be a good reason you want in."

"There is. Five good reasons, civilians and Emily Crockett."

Loomis nodded and walked away, leaving Bolan to his thoughts.

The soldier could have moved on, walked away and left the matter in the hands of others. But the Executioner was the one who could stand up for the innocents who were unable to fight back.

Later, back in his room, Bolan powered up the laptop he had borrowed from the hotel. It would allow him to view the contents of the flash drive Loomis had slipped into his jacket pocket as they had stood briefly at the grave of Jimmy Crocket. Loomis had brushed past the soldier as he moved away without a word being spoken, and Bolan had left in the other direction, returning to his hotel.

Sitting with the laptop on the small table, he let the computer power up. He inserted the flash drive into the USB port and waited while it installed itself. He tapped the keys to open the file and scrolled down: a number of mug shots, each with a short note identifying the individuals.

Harry Quintain was the local crew chief, a chubby-faced, balding guy in his mid-thirties. His sheet detailed his extensive criminal record.

Roy Soames was Quintain's broker-enforcer, a hard-looking guy with a lifelong rap sheet that had started when he was fourteen.

The files stated that Quintain handled illegal merchandise, including weapons, and had connections in Chicago, which was a distribution hub. Quintain ran the operation in Miami, but his allegiance was to the Chicago operation. It was suspected he moved around his local bases, using diverse locations, which meant law-enforcement agencies were having little success pinning them down.

For Bolan this was a beginning. The hard work lay ahead.

THE SOLDIER SPENT a couple of days watching the building that was Quintain's current base of operations. It was close to the ocean, a modern structure with plenty of glass and shiny steel. The elevator was one of those exposed models that ran up the front of the building so he was able to see Quintain, flanked by two bodyguards and Soames, enter the lobby and step into the elevator. Bolan counted off the floors and saw them step out on the ninth, where Quintain has his suite of offices. His observation of the building, though tedious, fed him what he wanted and by the afternoon of the third day Bolan had enough to make his move.

Quintain and Soames always arrived in separate cars but traveled together to the ninth floor via the elevator. Quintain spent his days in the building, while Soames made a couple of trips outside daily. Same time each day. He always left on his own, the bodyguards staying in the building with Quintain.

Bolan was ready on the third day, in his rental car, watching patiently. When Soames stepped out and crossed to his vehicle, Bolan fired up the engine and fell in behind the man as he exited the parking area. The soldier allowed a couple of cars between them.

They traveled for a good thirty minutes, Soames in no hurry, observing the speed limits. He was in a dark blue metallic Ferrari California convertible, an easy car to follow. Bolan stayed well behind. He saw Soames make a right, off the main drag and into an industrial park. The soldier carried on past the entrance, able to monitor Soames through the chain-link fence as he coasted along the line of storage units. A couple of hundred yards along Bolan spotted a service road, swung onto it and parked. He checked the 93-R in its holster under his sports coat, locked the rental and backtracked until he found a break in the poorly maintained perimeter fence.

Bolan stood for a moment as he fixed the last position of Soames's car, then moved steadily between the units as he closed in on the general area. It was plainly obvious the industrial area was deserted. Unit doors hung open. Windows, those not smashed, were dusty, which suited Bolan's purpose.

He picked up the sound of voices and tracked in toward them, the Beretta in his hand. Edging around the building, he spotted the Ferrari parked nose-in by a unit. The doors were open. A parked panel truck stood inside. Next to Soames's vehicle was a bright yellow Corvette.

He was in conversation with two men. One was well-dressed like Soames. The other had on denims and a florid silk shirt. The conversation appeared amiable.

Soames said something to the denim-clad man, who then went to the panel tuck and opened the rear doors, exposing a stack of long wooden crates. The top was removed from one of the crates and the guy lifted out an M240 7.62 mm machine gun. The weapon was strictly military ordnance, not designated for civilian use. It was a rapid-fire, belt-fed weapon and would prove devastatingly efficient in the hands of illegal users. Regular beat cops would have no defense against such a weapon if it got on the streets.

Soames checked the M240, nodding his approval. From what Bolan could see, Soames was the buyer, the other guy his source—which made him important to the Executioner.

Edging closer, Bolan was able to hear the conversation.

"You can get more?" Soames said.

"No problem."

Soames waved his hand at the guy holding the machine gun. "Pack them tight and deliver them to the pickup point." He took out a cell phone, tapped in a number and spoke. "Everything's okay. One dozen as requested. We can arrange final delivery. Let Cameron know. Yeah, Jake can get more." He closed the cell phone and dropped it in his pocket, turned and went to his car. He lifted out a leather satchel and handed it to his supplier. "Count it if you want, Jake."

The man called Jake hefted the satchel. "I can tell by the weight it's all there. And we trust each other, don't we, Roy? In this business, trust is everything."

Bolan allowed himself a tight smile. *Trust between scum.* That was a new concept.

"You'll tell your boss the deal went okay? Like I said, I can work out some sweet terms for you on future buys."

Soames nodded. "Don't see why not," he said, and tapped the satchel in Jake's hand. "Glad to get that cash off my hands."

"It's a lot of money," Jake said.

Bolan stepped into view, his Beretta covering the trio. "Let me take care of it for you," he said.

Jake stared at the soldier, his face expressionless. "Pal, you don't want to be doing this."

Soames's eyes blazed with anger, his cheeks coloring. "You know who I am, you fuck? Only thing that money will buy is your funeral. I work—"

"Roy, be advised that it doesn't pay to upset the guy holding a gun on you. And I know who you work for. I'm not impressed."

Soames's reaction, whether provoked by arrogance, or a need to maintain his credibility, was way off the charts. The

Executioner could only assume the man really believed he could deal with an adversary even under the threat of a gun.

The man went for the autopistol holstered at his hip, brushing aside the coat he was wearing, eyes widening with the surge of adrenaline that forced his action. His fingers brushed against the textured grips and got no further.

Bolan put a 9 mm triburst into his skull. The impact jerked Soames's head to one side and he fell back against the Ferrari, blood speckling the gleaming paintwork even as the man dropped to the dusty ground.

Behind him the denim-clad guy pulled his own weapon from his belt. It was a heavy revolver, and to his credit he brought it up quickly.

Not fast enough. Bolan had dropped to a crouch, swinging the muzzle of the 93-R in anticipation of the guy's move. He assumed a two-handed Weaver's stance, centering his target, and hit the guy in the chest. The thug stumbled back, falling half inside the open panel truck, legs jerking in spasms as the 9 mm slugs dug in deep. Bolan hit him with a second burst that burned in under the guy's chin and tore through to split his skull on exit.

Jake had turned on his heel and was moving for his own car when Bolan lunged forward. He hooked a hand in the weapons dealer's coat collar and swung him around. The Beretta made a solid, meaty sound as it slammed against Jake's jaw. The blow knocked him off his feet and he skidded on his knees into the side of the car. Then Bolan was standing over him, jabbing the hot muzzle of the Beretta into the man's cheek. Jake stared up into the glacial blue of the Executioner's eyes and saw his own terrified face reflected there.

"The bad things we do in life eventually catch up," Bolan said. "I'm not going to reflect on your misdemeanors. But I have a couple of questions, and I need fast answers."

Jake drew his sleeve across his torn and bloody jaw.

"Those two made wrong decisions and won't get a chance to clear their consciences. How about you, Jake?"

"What do you want?"

"Military ordnance. Where do you source it, Jake?"

"I'm a dead man if I talk."

"Look at me, Jake. Do I look as if care?"

The Beretta was pressed harder into his cheek.

"Time to think about yourself, Jake. Today isn't going to get any better."

"I can see that."

"Help me, Jake. My patience runs out fast. Who do you get your weapons from?"

"Guy in the military. Orin Cage. He's based at a main supply depot, in charge of weapons acquisition. He runs a little side-line business." The words began to tumble out almost as if Jake was in the confessional.

"Answer one question. Who do Soames and Quintain answer to?"

"Fredo Bella. He runs the Chicago division. Believe me, you don't want to screw with him. He's the boss in Chicago but even he works for a higher-up man who's based in New Mexico. There's also another guy in Chicago. Bella's paymaster, Guido Bertolli."

Jake quickly blurted out the rest of the information Bolan needed before lapsing into a sullen silence.

Bolan stepped back. "You work a dirty business, Jake. Nothing that could ever redeem itself in you."

"You got what you wanted. You happy?"

"Not exactly happy," Bolan said. "But at least satisfied for the moment." Then he hit the man on the side of his head with the butt of the Beretta, knocking him unconscious.

Bolan took the cell phone from Soames's pocket and put in a call to Miami-Dade PD. He told them where they could find the bodies and a consignment of stolen military hardware, plus a weapons dealer who was ready to talk. He also fed them the information about the Orin Cage and military connection, then cut the call. A search of Soames's jacket provided Bolan with a fat wallet and another cell phone. He put the items away for later examination and bent to pick up the satchel of money. It would help to finance his upcoming mission. He had a long drive ahead of him. Destination Chicago. The Windy City was going to experience an Executioner-style gale that would hope-fully sweep away some of its seedier trash.

Bolan made his way back to his parked rental and took the back roads until he was well clear of the area. He made a wide, circuitous drive back into Miami and his hotel. In his room he packed his belongings and called down to the desk, asking for his account to be readied for checkout.

He recalled the wallet he had taken from Soames's body and emptied the contents on the bed—a couple thousand in cash, multiple credit cards and a single business card. It told Bolan that Guido Bertolli worked out of Chicago with an office in the city. Bertolli's profession was financial adviser and his office address was displayed below his title, along with his telephone and cell number. Handy information, Bolan decided. It gave him a starting point once he reached Chicago.

Soames's cell phone offered nothing but a list of stored numbers. The one Bolan found interesting was listed under the name Quintain.

BOLAN MADE his call to Harry Quintain as he traveled the I-65 through Kentucky.

"Quintain, how's it going?"

"Who the fuck are you? How did you get this number?"

"From the late Roy Soames. I imagine you've already heard."

"You understand that wasn't a wise thing to do."

"Is this because I screwed a deal and lost your cargo to Miami PD?"

There was a considered silence. Bolan imagined Quintain working things through.

"I'll find you and kill everyone you care about," Quintain finally said.

Bolan thought about Stony Man and the people associated with it.

"Good luck with that," he said. "Just one last thing, Harry, I know where *you* live, too. One day I might come calling."

Bolan switched off the cell phone. A few miles farther on he exited the I-65 and drove into the small town he'd located. He parked close to the post office, wiped the cell phone clean of any prints and dropped it into the padded envelope he'd purchased earlier. It was addressed to Gary Loomis, Miami-Dade PD. Bolan went into the post office and mailed the envelope. Loomis might find the phone's contact numbers interesting. Even useful. The soldier stayed in the town long enough to have a meal before rejoining the interstate and continuing his journey.

He had checked the distance to Chicago after leaving his hotel. Miami to Chicago was around thirteen hundred miles, a run of approximately twenty hours. Bolan made it in easy stages, with a motel break to catch up on sleep. He placed a single cell phone call from his room and made contact with Barbara Price.

"You still on R & R?"

There was a hint of something more than just asking about his health.

"Shouldn't I be?" Bolan said.

"Let's say a certain incident in Miami aroused my interest."

"Incident?"

"The kind that sort of has your signature on it. Something I should know about?"

"This is not an SOG issue," Bolan said. "Flying solo. But I need to talk to the Bear."

"Okay. Hey, you watch your back, soldier. You want to reconsider the lone-wolf status on this one?"

"Thanks, but no, thanks. This is something I need to do without dragging you guys in."

"Kind of personal, huh?"

"Kind of."

"I'll patch you through."

"Catch up with you later."

Bolan heard the soft click as the call was transferred to

Aaron "the Bear" Kurtzman's cyber lair. A moment later the recognizable, gruff sound of Kurtzman's voice came on.

"Hey, big guy, haven't heard from you in a while. You having an extended vacation?"

"Not any longer," Bolan said. "I need some intel."

"Sure," Kurtzman said. "So what can I do for you?"

"Find out background details on a Chicago lowlife named Fredo Bella, head honcho in the trafficking of stolen arms in the area. A source said Bella's strings are pulled by a Lou Cameron based in New Mexico. I'm driving to Chicago in the morning, so call my cell when you get the goods. I also need intel on a guy by the name of Guido Bertolli. According to his business card, he runs a financial advisory service in the city. Could be legit, but I found it in the wallet of a dirtbag named Roy Soames. And information I got suggested Bertolli is linked to Bella. I just need you to confirm."

"You got it, Striker. Anything else?"

"No," Bolan said. "Just the intel. And pictures if you can find them. Leave it until morning if you get anything. And thanks."

"Anytime."

Bolan put the cell phone on charge before he turned in. Last thing he needed was the phone going dead on him if Kurtzman was trying to send him information.

"YOU PICKED a prize specimen," Kurtzman said over the cell phone.

Bolan was eating breakfast in the diner down the road from the motel. "So enlighten me," he said.

"Fredo Bella. He's forty-two years old and heads up one hell of an organized crime business. Arms dealing is one page in his dossier. The guy will buy and sell anything as long as he can make a profit. This is a slippery character, Striker. The Chicago PD and the Feds have been on his case for years, but the man knows the game too well. He's lawyered up to the ears. Pays very well and expects the best protection. He's been charged a number of times, but nothing ever gets beyond that.

The guy's been suspected of a couple of homicides, and I stress the word 'suspected' as in legally. CPD *know* he did them, but they haven't been able to take it any further. Witnesses have a habit of disappearing, if you get my drift. And Bertolli does have connections with Bella. Looks like he could be the local money guy for the organization."

"Understood. That's the intel I got myself."

"There's a little more you might be interested in. Bella may be the hotshot in the Midwest, but he does dance to Lou Cameron's tune. These guys are so connected it's like an old-style Mafia Family."

"Well, we know what happened to them, don't we?"

Kurtzman's rumbling chuckle made Bolan smile.

"You take care, Striker. These people have bad reputations. I kid you not."

"Thanks for the warning."

"Pictures are coming through when we finish speaking. Anything else?"

"Background on this Cameron and his outfit might be helpful."

"Leave it with me," Kurtzman said. "Oh, and Fredo Bella has a number of properties in and around Chicago. His main residence…"

2

Fredo Bella's main residence was a 2,500-square-foot apartment in a glittering steel-and-glass high-rise situated on Chicago's North Lakeshore Drive. On the southwest corner of the building the apartment looked out over the city skyline and also had a view across the lake. According to Kurtzman's intel, the apartment cost in the region of $1.5 million. Probably small change to Bella.

Like many career criminals, Bella, who viewed the law with distaste, had a penchant for flaunting his wealth. He was confident enough to show the results of his illegal operations because he felt secure, untouchable. He surrounded himself with legal battalions and bought favors from those in high places.

Bolan located the building on his arrival in Chicago. His drive by was just a recon. He parked up short of the apartment building, looking it over. He liked to know where his quarry was based. He had no hard and fast plans for the man's home yet. The Executioner was more interested in Bella's operations. He was hoping that a visit to Guido Bertolli's office might give him that information.

GREGOR LEMINOV was far from happy, despite the luxurious surroundings of Fredo Bella's apartment. The Russian *Mafiya* broker was not in good humor. In the past half hour he had ordered his burly bodyguard to pour him two more glasses of

Bella's expensive whiskey and had quickly downed each tumbler in hefty gulps.

The heavyset Russian stared out through the apartment's panoramic windows, watching sheets of rain sweep in from Lake Michigan and slam against the glass. The gray clouds over the choppy water matched his mood, and the longer he had to wait, the worse his mood became. Leminov snapped his fingers and held out his glass.

"I might as well drink his liquor," he said to Mikhail Rostov, his personal bodyguard.

Rostov, who would never drink while he was on duty, took the tumbler and refilled it. He handed it to his boss, then resumed his position close by.

"Is taking a long time, boss," Rostov said.

"Always one to state the obvious, Mikhail. In this case you are right." Leminov sat forward. "Perhaps it is time to remind our host how long we have been waiting."

The double doors to the spacious room swung open then, and Fredo Bella strode through, a beaming smile on his rounded face.

"Gregor, my friend." He noticed the almost empty glass in Leminov's large hand. "Let me fix you another drink. What would you like?"

"An explanation would be nice. Fredo, where are Mr. Poliokof's machine guns?"

Bella sat behind his curving pale wood desk. The heavy executive chair creaked as Bella's weight put it under some strain. The man was six feet tall, and carried a lot of weight. Even his hand-tailored Versace suit failed to hide his soft bulk. He was a big man with big appetites.

"No crap, Gregor. I'm nothing if not truthful. There was an incident in Florida. Somebody, and I don't know who yet, showed up at the exchange. He killed my guy, Soames, and took out the driver of the van. He took off with the cash, as well."

"What about the weapons?"

Bella dug a finger inside his shirt collar, where it suddenly started to dig into his neck. "Worst fuckin' part," he said. "The son of a bitch went and called the cops in. Miami PD have the M240s in their lockup, along with the delivery guy. I am not worried about him, though. His knowledge is limited."

Leminov felt a compulsion to drain his glass of whiskey. As he held it up for a refill, Rostov stepped forward and took it.

"So everything has gone and the deal falls flat. I have to tell Mr. Poliokof he doesn't get his weapons?"

Bella held up a hand. "No, Gregor. The guns will be delivered. A fresh shipment. That takes time. It may be a little late, but the weapons *will* be delivered." He cleared his throat, forcing words out that plainly hurt to utter. "You won't be out of pocket. I'll stand the loss. It was my end of the deal, so I'll take the hit."

This time Leminov sipped the whiskey slowly, savoring it as much as he savored Bella's offer.

"Look, Gregor, we've been doing business for a good few years. This is the first time something like this has happened. I've got my people on it. They're looking for this bastard. We'll find him, and when I get my hands on him he'll beg to be killed."

"Before you do, ask him what he did with the money."

"If he's spent it, I'll strip it out of his flesh."

"I wish you luck with that. This man sounds extremely capable. He's not a reckless crackhead."

Bella shrugged. "I didn't get where I am by luck. Everything I've got is due to hard work. This asshole isn't going to get the better of me."

"I think he already did." Leminov leaned forward, his voice lowering. "Be as casual as you like, Fredo. Just remember who you are dealing with. You do not want to upset Mr. Poliokof. In business he accepts no excuses. Late delivery is late delivery. All I say is this will be marked against you."

"Christ, Gregor, what am I supposed to do? Snap my fingers and make the fucking guns appear like magic? Poliokof is going to have to wait. Okay?"

Leminov took out his cell phone and hit a number. He stared impassively across the room as he waited. When his call was answered he lapsed into Russian, leaving Bella to wonder what was being said. He completed the call and snapped his phone shut.

"So?" Bella asked.

"Mr. Poliokof is not happy. You lose the guns. You lose the money. Delivery is delayed. Nothing is resolved. He is angry that you make him wait. Mr. Poliokof is not the kind of man you disrespect like this. He warns you this is not the end of the matter."

"Gregor, I have other clients. The only merchandise I have at the moment has already been sold to someone else. It's due for pickup. When that goes, the pot is empty. Your order was next. Since it's gone, I have to wait for *my* contact to bulk up on stock. Poliokof will have to stand in line until I can sort things out. He's not the fucking President of the United States. Simple terms, Gregor. If I don't have it, I can't supply it."

Leminov gave a slight shrug. "Then it will have to be. I will pass your remarks to Mr. Poliokof. Then we see what happens." He pushed to his feet and crossed to the door. As he went through he said, "Watch out for yourself, Fredo."

And then he was gone, his bodyguard trailing after him.

Next Morning.

"BERTOLLI IS THEIR paymaster," Zader Poliokof said. "Maybe he can help us out with our cash problem. Find him, take him somewhere you won't be disturbed and have a talk with him."

"A friendly talk?" Leminov said.

"Of course. We are not animals, Gregor. Allow him his say. Within reason."

"He may not be all that willing to cooperate."

"Then make him realize he has no choice," Poliokof stated.

"I can see this having a less than pleasant outcome."

Poliokof smiled. "If it happens, it happens."

Midafternoon.

FREDO BELLA PICKED UP the phone. "Yeah? What do you mean he isn't around?"

"He's not at his office, boss. We checked his apartment. He isn't there, either."

"Okay. I got the exchange tonight. Check around and see if anyone knows where he is. Go back to his office. Bring his laptop to me at the site," Bella said. "No excuses on this, Jerry. Until we know where Bertolli is, I want those codes safe."

"No problem, boss. Hey, boss, what do you think happened to him?"

"I'm working on it. You just concentrate on finding him."

3

Bolan found Bertolli's building and parked in the alley, then walked back to the front and entered the lobby. It was an old building, with few modern electronics. He paused at the indicator board and read off the list of offices and companies. *Bertolli—Financial Adviser* was on the third floor. Bolan climbed the stairs. He could hear business being conducted behind the closed doors of the offices he passed—the occasional sound of telephones, people chattering.

He reached the third floor and walked the corridor until he came to the door he wanted. The carpet underfoot was worn and dusty. It was obvious that Bertolli had maintained a low profile, conducting his dealings for Bella in seclusion. His financial advice business concealed his involvement in more lucrative operations.

The door, with its frosted glass upper panel, was in keeping with the rest of the building. Bolan grasped the handle and put his hip against the wooden frame, feeling the inner lock give after the third solid thrust. He held the door, glancing round. The corridor was empty. The soldier eased the door open and slipped inside, closing it behind him.

The office decor was impersonal and drab: one desk with a leather swivel seat, shelves holding box files, a row of filing cabinets, a couple of wooden chairs lined up against a wall. Bolan crossed to the desk, which held only a few office items—a phone, a desk pad.

Bolan checked the desk drawers. In the second one down he found an expensive laptop. He slid it out, then closed the drawer and straightened.

And looked at the muzzle of a pistol aimed at him.

There were two men, young and hard-faced. The one by the door had the look of the leader, and he had a hefty pistol in one hand. The other guy, who was holding the pistol on Bolan, had a faint smirk on his angular face.

"Naughty, naughty," he crowed. "It's illegal to break into someone's office and steal things."

"I'll try not to lose sleep over it," Bolan said.

"Should I rap him in the mouth?"

The guy at the door said, "No, Rick, but you should check him for a weapon."

"Yeah," the gunner said, and proceeded to feel under Bolan's coat. He withdrew the Beretta. "You got a license to carry this?"

Bolan resisted the urge to make another smart reply. There was a gleam in the guy's eyes that told him this one was less in control than his partner.

"You think he's a cop?"

"No."

"Fed of some kind. I don't like Feds."

"Only their mothers like Feds."

The gunner dropped the Beretta into a side pocket of his jacket and flicked his head at Bolan.

"Let's go," he said before scooping up the laptop and stepping up close behind Bolan.

The guy by the door opened it and checked the corridor.

"Out," he said. "Turn left and make for the fire exit at the end of the hall."

The exit door was unlocked and Bolan was escorted through and down the iron fire escape fixed to the outer wall. It took them to a small parking lot, at the rear of the building.

Bolan watched as the laptop was placed inside a late-model

Ford. He was considering his options, trying to place himself ahead of the game.

"We taking a ride?" he asked, directing his question at the lead guy.

"We've got what we came for, plus you," the man said. He was looking pleased with himself. "You're a bonus. The boss is going to be happy seeing you. Maybe you can tell him where Bertolli is."

"Why should I know? He's the guy I was looking for myself."

"Rick, check him over again in case he has a backup."

Bolan let the guy frisk him. They had his 93-R. It was his only weapon, but the pair was smart enough to make sure for themselves.

"He's clean," Rick said, disappointment in his tone.

"Hand me his pistol," the lead guy said.

Rick passed it over.

"Thought I recognized it." He inspected the Beretta, balancing it in his hand. "Nice piece," he said with genuine appreciation.

Rick glanced at it. "It's just a fuckin' gun, Jerry. Don't go getting a hard-on for it."

"You think? This is a Beretta 93-R, an Italian masterpiece. There's a setting on the selector that let's you fire three-round bursts. How many other semiautos can do that?"

Jerry's partner waggled his head. "Big whoop."

"Rick, being a moron isn't enough for you. You prove it every time you open your mouth."

"Hey! There's no call for that. I ain't that dumb. Who got the blonde piece everyone was after the other night? Huh? Go on, tell me. Well, it wasn't you, Beretta man."

Jerry shook his head. "Just like I said, Rick, dumb as ever. Stop thinking with your dick and use your brain for a change."

Rick stared at his partner for long seconds, concentration screwing up his face. Then he decided Jerry *was* belittling him, and he leaned forward to swipe at Jerry's arm. "Cut that out…"

He didn't finish. In fact those three words were the last he ever spoke.

Bolan moved, using the thin window of opportunity, and caught hold of Rick's extended arm. He propelled the guy forward into Jerry, following through to slam his right elbow down into the back of Rick's neck. The blow was hard, driving the guy to his knees. Before Rick hit the concrete Bolan had moved on, gripping Jerry's gun arm and forcing it down. Jerry's finger jerked the trigger and the pistol fired with a hard bang. The slug cored into the back of Rick's skull, exiting through his face and blowing bloody gore onto the ground. Bolan drove the palm of his right hand up into Jerry's face, crushing his nose. Blood squirted in bright streams. The sudden pain drained Jerry's resistance, and he uttered a strangled moan. The Executioner hit him again, going for the man's throat, knuckles driving into soft flesh and crushing everything in its path. Jerry gagged, dropping both guns he was holding, and clawed at his ruined throat, desperately trying to suck in air that wasn't coming. He fell back against the side of the car as Bolan picked up the dropped Beretta. He stepped back and fired a single shot into Jerry's skull, silencing him completely.

The soldier slid the Beretta into its shoulder holster, then went through the dead men's pockets. They were carrying very little—some loose cash and a cell phone from Jerry's leather jacket.

Bolan crossed to the car and slid inside. The laptop lay where Rick had placed it. Noticing a GPS unit mounted on the dash, he turned on the ignition and powered up the unit, checking on the current setting. The small screen illustrated a route that had been entered recently, according to the time readout. It might offer Bolan a destination. He detached the GPS unit from the dash, unplugged it from the power source and took it, along with the laptop, with him.

Back in his own car Bolan set the GPS unit on the dash panel and turned it on. The recent settings still showed. He took the cell phone he'd found and checked it out. No voice calls, but there were a couple of text messages. Bolan opened them. The first was a text from the cell phone provider, offering Jerry free credits. The soldier went to the second, most recent message. It had been received no more than a half hour ago. The text advised Jerry to enter the coordinates that followed into his GPS and to drive the route. They were expected within the next hour. At the end of the message was a single name— Bella. When Bolan checked the coordinates from the text they matched the ones entered into the GPS unit.

He started the car and drove out of the lot, following the screen directions and the female voice backup. He had no idea where he was going to end up, but if it brought him to Fredo Bella it was going to be worth the trip.

The journey lasted almost forty-five minutes. Though the dark and the rain made it difficult for Bolan to know where this trip was taking him, he was aware of the less than pleasant landscape as he drove down poorly illuminated streets, with rundown buildings on either side. There were abandoned cars. Shuttered windows. Then he was entering what would have been a busy industrial section of the city at one time, but urban decay had taken hold, leaving only blackened, abandoned buildings.

Bolan recalled what Jerry had said about Bertolli. It was plain the man had gone missing, and his disappearance was a mystery to Bella's people. Maybe Bolan could figure it out later.

The soldier followed the GPS as it led him deeper into the industrial wasteland. The voice told him he was within a few hundred yards of his journey's end. He swung the car into the deep shadows of an open-ended structure that had rusted, overgrown steel rails leading inside. He killed the engine and sat, hearing only the heavy rain on the corrugated roof above him.

Jerry and Rick had been ordered to meet with Bella at this location. Bolan was certain it wasn't an invitation to a wine tasting.

Something was happening.

Imminently.

Bolan decided to crash the party.

Exiting the car, he raised the trunk and slipped off his outer clothing, revealing his blacksuit underneath. A black baseball cap completed his uniform. From his war bag he chose his weapons and checked their loads. He slipped a compact, powerful monocular into a pocket, closed the trunk and locked the car, placing the key in one of his blacksuit's secure pockets. The GPS had shown that his destination lay directly to his right. Bolan followed the route, working his way silently through the gloom and the steady downpour. The falling rain would cover his movements and any peripheral sound he might make.

He spotted his destination through the downpour—a haze of light at first, then as he closed in, he made out the dark bulk of the building. Open doors showed him movement inside. Bolan edged closer, using the scatterings of industrial debris as cover as he moved in.

Bolan took out the monocular and focused in on the open doors of the building. He spotted vehicles, men moving back and forth, lifting wooden crates from the largest truck and distributing them between the smaller vehicles. There was enough illumination for him to be able to identify the size and shape of the boxes, even down to the military markings on them.

He saw a number of the men carrying weapons as they kept an eye on the proceedings.

A single, armed sentry covered the exterior, and overseeing the operation was the man himself.

Fredo Bella, in his expensive clothing, dominated the scene as he issued orders.

The darkness cloaked Bolan, the persistent rain matching his mood. He crouched close to his target, a chill wind tugging at his blacksuit. The sprawl of industrial buildings, long abandoned, served the predators who had no idea the Executioner was about to descend upon them and reduce their business to ashes. Inside the derelict structure they handled their illegal merchandise, preparing to ship out the weapons for the deals they had already made, none of them realizing the fury already making his move to close them down.

As he eased up behind the lone sentry by the entrance, Bolan

wiped cold rain from his eyes with his sleeve, ignoring the keen
slice of the wind scything across the compound. He adjusted
the M-16 A-2 across his back where it hung alongside his regular 9 mm Uzi, reaching down to free the Cold Steel Tanto knife
from its sheath at his waist. The black blade offered no reflection as Bolan rose to his full height behind the sentry.

The Executioner was a black-clad wraith fully armed for
what lay ahead.

The sentry felt the strong fingers that pushed the cap from
his head and curled into his hair, yanking his head back, then
drew breath as the keen edge of the knife etched across his taut
throat. It bit deeply, severing everything in its path, releasing
a surge of warm blood that spilled down over his waterproof
jacket. He struggled in wordless agony, held upright by Bolan's
powerful grip until his strength dissipated along with his spilled
blood. Only when the sentry ceased to struggle did Bolan allow
him to slump to his knees, then onto his face. The man was still
in spasm as the soldier stepped over him and paused briefly at
the entrance. He loosened the M-16, peering inside the opening
before he stepped through into the dimly lit interior. Crouching
against the wall, lost in the deep shadows there, Bolan surveyed
the scene, spotting a ragged line of heavy steel containers. He
eased along the wall until the containers provided him with a
wall of protection.

From there he was able to view the operation at close quar-
ters.

Two dilapidated panel trucks were parked beneath a bank of
pallid fluorescent lights. A number of men were busy checking and loading cases from a third, larger vehicle, distributing them between the panel trucks. Bolan located an expensive
late-model BMW nearby, the gleaming paintwork speckled
with raindrops.

Even as he looked over the situation, Bolan's hands were
checking his handguns, the 9 mm Beretta 93-R in his shoulder
rig, the big Magnum Desert Eagle resting snugly in the high
ride holster on his right hip. He carried extra magazines for
each handgun, as well as for the M-16 and Uzi, in the combat

harness over the blacksuit. In addition he carried a number of flash-bang grenades and M-34 phosphorous grenades.

Satisfied his intel was sound, Bolan eased off the M-16's safety, selecting the triburst setting. He freed one of the flash-bang grenades, pulled the pin, then threw the canister so hard that it landed in between the parked panel trucks. Bolan opened his mouth, shielded his ears and turned his head away from the harsh burst of sound and white light as the grenade detonated. Men yelled in surprise and pain as they staggered back from the blast. Someone, perhaps shielded from the effects of the grenade, opened fire and Bolan heard slugs clanging off the metalwork around him. Angry shouts erupted.

Still crouching, the Executioner shouldered the M-16 and picked his targets. The tribursts from his rifle set up echoing noise. A man cried out as 5.56 mm slugs found his vulnerable flesh. Bolan swept the M-16's muzzle back and forth, following targets and dropping a couple more before the main group found cover behind the parked vehicles and began to fire back.

"Spread," a voice commanded. "Don't give him easy targets."

Figures fanned out across the floor, seeking shelter so make-shift firing positions could be established. Return fire was concentrated on Bolan's position, the steel wall rejecting the hard slam of autofire. The soldier edged along the line of containers until he was clear of his original spot, then raised himself and opened fire again. He heard someone cursing, followed by the clatter of a dropped weapon. More voices called out. Bolan detected traces of panic in some of the words and allowed a thin smile to edge his lips.

He freed one of the M-34 phosphorous grenades, pulled the pin and tossed the bomb in the direction of one of the panel trucks. His aim turned out to be better than he might have imagined. The grenade landed inside the open rear doors, rolling to rest against the stacked cargo. One of the men saw it and made the mistake of scrambling inside the truck to retrieve the grenade. It detonated in the moment his fingers grasped it. The guy let out a harsh scream as the phosphorous burned its way into his flesh, gnawing deep into the bone. Howling in agony, the man was consumed as the phosphorous expanded, filling the truck interior with a blinding surge of incandescent heat that would reach 5,000° F. At the point where the stored ammunition began to ignite, the panel truck was blown apart, the stripped metal panels adding to misery being heaped upon the armed group, slivers of razor-sharp steel scything in all directions. Some of those fragments caught vulnerable flesh and men went to their knees in pain.

Bolan used the distraction to add his own brand of justice, the autorifle pumping out tribursts that took more of the men down. He replaced his empty magazine with a fresh one and kept up his steady fire, punching the shooters down as they attempted to take him out. It turned into an uneven contest. Bolan, despite the shots fired in his direction, continued to mop up.

Out the corner of his eye he saw a bulky, suited figure break free from cover, clearing the drifting smoke from the blown truck, and running in the direction of the BMW. Someone was leaving the party. Even in that brief moment, Bolan recognized Fredo Bella from the mug shot Kurtzman had sent him. The soldier swung the M-16 around, working the lever for single shots. He tracked his target and fired, the 5.56 mm slug impacting against the Bella's right thigh, shattering bones. The Executioner followed with a second shot that cored into the man's left leg and toppled him facedown on the grimy floor.

As the sound of the final shots faded, the silence broken only by the moans coming from Bella, Bolan checked out the area. Only when he was convinced the battle was over did he move from cover and inspect the other parked vehicles and their contents. He discovered a generous selection of weapons that included automatic rifles and automatic pistols, as well as a plentiful supply of ammunition for the various pieces. In one van he located a case of military Light Anti-Tank Weapons—LAWs. Bolan's concern rose at the sight of the shoulder-launched missiles. The ordnance was destined for street gangs—urban crime. Automatic weapons were bad enough, but the inclusion of LAWs took the concept of street violence to a new level. It convinced Bolan that his intel had not been exaggerated. His foray here in Chicago was more than justified.

Bolan broke open one of the LAW boxes and lifted out three of the launchers, slinging them from his shoulder. Additional ordnance was always welcome. Backing off, he primed and dropped more M-34s into the remaining vehicles, including the BMW. With the grenades burning down their fuses, Bolan made a swift retreat and ducked for cover seconds before the grenades ignited and the fearsome burst of phosphorous threw out heat that turned the vehicles into blazing wrecks. The crackling sound of igniting ammunition echoed around the building. Smoke and fire followed in their wake.

Bolan exited as swiftly and silently as he had made his entrance, his work in the Windy City done for the moment. The people who ordered the weapons were going to be sorely disappointed. The Executioner's work for this dark night was over.

The soldier worked his way out of the area, back to where he had parked his rental, he fished the key from a zip pocket, opened the trunk and placed his weapons inside. He pulled his civilian clothing back over his blacksuit, then donned a cord jacket. Taking his Beretta, he stowed it under the driver's seat and fired up the engine. He nosed out of the shed and drove away from the battle zone, retracing the route he had used to come in. When he was several minutes away, he picked up the approaching sound of police cruisers. Bolan held his speed as he eased back to the main thoroughfare. He had reached a busy intersection when a couple of CPD cruisers sped by, followed by ambulances and a fire truck.

Twenty minutes later Bolan parked in the basement garage of his hotel, backing the rental into a slot. He locked the vehicle and picked up a leather attaché case from the rear seat. He dropped the Beretta into the case along with the laptop, slipped on the dark topcoat he'd kept on the seat and made his way from the garage to the hotel entrance. As he crossed the lobby, the lone woman behind the desk glanced up. She studied him for a moment, then smiled.

"Late finish?" she said as Bolan requested his key card.

"Corporate takeovers have no concept of time," he said, giving her a friendly grin. "Some people just don't know when to give in."

"Room service is still available, Mr. Cooper. Can I arrange for something to be sent up?"

"Coffee and sandwiches would be nice," Bolan said.

The woman stared into the warm blue eyes and decided that Mr. Cooper was a nice man. "Well, I hope your evening was successful."

Mack Bolan nodded briefly. "It was," he said. "Extremely productive."

BOLAN PLUGGED the laptop into the room's electrical outlet, powered it up and watched as the wireless internet connection set up. He opened the program and studied the saved files. They appeared to be in some kind of code that defeated Bolan's limited IT skills. He used his cell phone to call Stony Man Farm. The call was eventually routed to the Computer Room, and he explained his problem to Akira Tokaido.

"No problem," the computer hacker said. "Let me download those files and I'll take a look."

Bolan's room service order arrived, so he left Tokaido to his computer code breaking. He had barely finished when his cell phone rang.

"Nothing difficult, Striker. The guy used a simple coding scheme to hide his files. Overseas bank accounts. Usual stuff. Some big amounts of money being handled here. I could quit and live off the interest these guys are making."

"Anything else?"

"Telephone numbers, contact list, delivery dates."

"Current details?"

"I can only tell you what I see. I can't make sense of any of it."

"Just give me what you have," Bolan said. "You're doing fine."

"Latest information has an upcoming transaction at South Auto Salvage in Newark. Due midnight tomorrow."

"You got any information on who runs South Auto Salvage?"

"Nicky Costanza. I checked him out. He's a career criminal who's into all kinds of rackets. Not a nice dude."

"If they were all nice dudes, Akira, we'd be out of a job."

"I guess so. I'll transfer the information to your laptop. With pictures and GPS coordinates to land you right at South Auto Salvage's front door."

"Thanks for this," Bolan said. "Tell Aaron I said you can have a raise."

Tokaido laughed. "Do I get that in writing?"

"You wish."

4

McQueen County, New Mexico

Tony Lorenzo watched Lou Cameron's eyes. He knew his boss well enough to be wary. Cameron had a mercurial capacity for mood changes. He could lash out in an instant, not giving a damn who he hurt in the process, and bad news was a sure way of incurring the man's wrath. Lorenzo had seen Cameron kill without hesitation because something had gone off track. He struck out in a simple reflex reaction to setbacks. So bringing Cameron the information about the hit on the Chicago deal was a risky piece of business. Which was why Lorenzo studied the expression in Cameron's eyes very carefully.

As usual, Cameron was dressed in a well-cut suit and a white shirt open at the collar. Tall, with a lean build, he looked more like a banker on a break than a career criminal who had graduated from petty crime to his position as a premier supplier of illegal arms. With his youthful, handsome good looks and sandy hair, Cameron could have earned a good living as an actor. The letdown was his eyes. They were sharp and cold, the kind that instilled caution in anyone thinking of defying him.

A brief silence followed the report. As Cameron's hand gripped the whiskey bottle, his knuckles turned white. It was the only indication of his anger. He leaned forward and filled the tumbler, placed the bottle on the glass table, then sat back with the drink in his hand. It was very quiet in the room. Not one of the six men present wanted to be the first to speak.

"Has anyone figured out who made the hit?" Cameron asked. "Cops? Feds? Some local opposition?"

"Bella was the only survivor. He was pretty badly cut up and burned, and had slugs in both legs. He came through with some information when our contact visited, but all we got was a single hitter," Lorenzo said, "well-armed, dressed in black and knew exactly what he was doing. Like he came out of nowhere. He took out the guard, then went inside the warehouse and blew everything all to hell. Used some kind of phosphorous grenades to burn up the merchandise."

"Then it doesn't sound like local cops or the Feds. They go to the fuckin' john in pairs. And destroying evidence doesn't fit the rule book."

"If it *was* a local hit, why would they wipe out the merchandise?" one of the group asked. "That was a high-price consignment."

Cameron nodded. "Good point. Let's check this out. Contact Chicago. Get some muscle to make the rounds—kick down some doors and bruise some asses. Spread some money. Find out who this joker might be and if he does work for somebody. If it turns out to be some home group, they're dead." He tossed back the whiskey and waved a dismissive hand. "Let's go, people."

"You figure this is the same guy who hit the exchange in Miami?" someone asked. "Can't be a coincidence coming so close together."

"We have to consider they might be connected," Cameron admitted, "which is why we get local people on the streets asking questions and pushing hard."

The man who had asked about the destruction of the consignment said, "If we get our hands on this guy, do we put him out of his misery? Or do you want to talk to him?"

"Oh, I want to talk to him. Now, I don't mind if he gets a little bruised on the way, but I want him breathing and able to speak. Let's get to it, boys."

Lorenzo waited until the room had cleared. He closed the heavy door and turned to face Cameron.

"Pretty expensive mess, Lou," he said. "The cargo in Miami and now Chicago. Vehicles. Bella's BMW, still with the new-leather smell. And seven of our guys."

Cameron nodded, waiting. When Lorenzo didn't continue, he said, "Bella ran the Chicago team. He shouldn't have let this happen. He got sloppy and paid the price. What concerns me more is the way this is going to look. Two hits like this is a loss of face."

"Yeah, well, I didn't want to push it too far by mentioning that."

Cameron slumped back in his leather armchair, drumming his fingers on the padded arms. His eyes wandered around the expensively decorated room.

"Can I have a drink?" Lorenzo asked, a slight hesitation in his tone.

"Go ahead." Cameron watched his man fill a tumbler and take a swallow. "Hey, you know how much that stuff is a bottle? I'm only asking because the way you're slopping it down it might as well be tap water."

"Yeah. I must be nervous," Lorenzo said. "I get like that when I start adding up cash loss."

Cameron smiled. "Tony, forget that. We can stand the loss from Miami and Chicago. It's a pain in the butt, sure, but I'm more concerned about the how and the why. I don't give a damn about Soames's spot. He isn't that important. Just a middleman. But Bella's warehouse was supposed to be safe. That's our part of the hood. Like church grounds. Consecrated. Off-limits. No one walks in off the fucking street and takes down one of my places."

"Looks like this guy didn't know that."

"That's stating the obvious. So this is how we play it. I want you to take charge, Tony. I mean the whole nine yards in Chicago. You're the new boss. If anybody doesn't like it, you get them to talk to me. Get things back on track. Make your mark, Tony. You earned this."

"Thanks, Lou, I won't let you down."

"Kick some ass up there. Remind those assholes who they work for, and don't take any crap. It's your priority—drop everything else. Choose a couple of guys to do the running for you, but get me results."

Lorenzo drained his glass, then cleared his throat. "What about Calvera?"

"I'll handle him. He won't be happy when I tell him his order isn't going to be delivered for a few more days, but he's going to have to suck it up."

"Let's hope *he* sees it that way."

Cameron raised his hands. "Shit happens, Tony. He'll get over it. I took the hit, not him."

"Okay."

As Lorenzo headed for the door Cameron said, "One thing needs clearing up soon as. Bella. This mess is down to him, so he's no longer of any use to me. He screwed up big, and he might start to open his mouth if the cops start coming around. Make it so the only way he leaves the hospital is via the morgue. Understand?"

"Consider it done," Lorenzo said, and then left the room.

Finally on his own, Cameron stared at the phone. Make the fucking call, he told himself. What the hell is José Calvera going to do? Sue me? He smiled at his own joke, reached out to tap in the number and waited for the call to be picked up.

The moment Calvera picked up and spoke, Cameron knew the bad news had already reached him. His Hispanic temperament always got the better of him, and he launched into a loud rant over the delay in getting his order. Cameron allowed the man to get it out of his system.

"I got a fuckin' street war in the making," Calvera concluded. "You know the score here. The *federales* are hitting us hard. Our rival cartels are bustin' my *cojones* trying to take over. I want my boys armed so they don't get wiped out on the first day. You promised me, Lou. Now you tell me my delivery is delayed because you got some shit happening in Chicago."

"This thing kind of held me up. I need to calm things down

for a day or two. Let me handle it, José, and I'll have your stuff on the way soon as possible."

"Don't let me down. If I get angry over this, we are going to have our own war. Do you understand me, amigo?"

"José, take a breath. You'll get your stuff soon enough. You know that. I honor my deals. All I ask is a couple more days and you'll have your consignment. I'll even throw in a few extra items as compensation for your trouble. Is that fair?"

Slightly mollified, Calvera grunted in agreement.

"So what happened?"

"Some kind of screwup with merchandise. I've got my hands full sorting it out. My crew boss in Chicago fucked up, so Tony Lorenzo is on his way there. He's the new boss. The other guy is out."

Calvera chuckled. "Hey, this is me you're talking to, Lou. I already heard about the problem in Chicago. Screwup with merchandise? You got hit, and your weapons were blown to hell. Tell me I'm wrong, amigo."

"José, nothing gets by you, huh? Yeah, I got hit. Miami, too. So things are a little crazy at the moment."

"Who is responsible?" Calvera asked.

"As of yet I have no idea. The smoke has hardly had time to settle, but I'm going to find out."

"Maybe you have a new player trying to move in on your territory," Calvera said.

"Anything is possible, Jose. What's certain is the son of a bitch who did this will be more than sorry he screwed with Louis Cameron."

"Maybe he doesn't realize who you are."

"I'm about to change that," Cameron stated.

"So I hear from you soon? *Sí?*"

"Muy pronto, mi amigo."

Cameron cut the call and sat back. He didn't even look up when the door opened and someone stepped into the room and crossed to his desk. He knew who his visitor was. The familiar drag of one foot against the floor told him it was Nathan, his younger brother.

"I can quote you down to the last dime how much that Chicago mess cost us," Nathan said. "I've just been working it out."

Cameron had to smile. Only Nathan could do that, work out the potential loss to the final dot.

"Little bro," he said, "I just knew you'd come up with something like that."

"Yeah, well, it isn't like I have a lot else to do."

Nathan eased himself into one of the chairs by the desk. At twenty-nine he was five years younger than his brother, whip thin, with dark good looks, his hair worn shoulder length. He dressed well and expensively. His left leg was thrust out stiffly, and his lips tightened in reaction to the ache that never seemed to fully go away. The leg had been badly damaged in the aftermath of a horrific auto accident when he was eighteen. Five people had died in the crash, the result of a head-on collision on the local highway. Nathan, a passenger, had been cut from the wreck after three hours. He had been the only survivor. Despite the surgery that saved his leg, he was left disabled and in pain that came and went. No amount of aftercare restored the damaged limb. But Nathan endured because he had no choice. He'd turned to drugs to dull the pain and might have succumbed all the way if his brother had not stepped in. Lou's intervention kept his younger brother from losing it completely. He brought him into the organization and put him in charge of running the financial side of the business. Nathan had a natural aptitude for money matters, and he had never taken a wrong step when it came to organizing the cash flow.

"Hey, bro, how are we feeling today?"

Nathan massaged his leg. "Kicked off this morning and won't let up," he said. "Hey, I know you got problems. I don't want to make a fuss."

"You'll have me crying in a minute," Lou said, his tone light as he chided his brother.

"You're a mean mother."

"That's me," Lou said with a big grin. "So, am I going to need to sell off one of my cars to make up the loss?"

"That would make you cry. The money is just a drop in the pool, but what the fuck is going on, Lou? Who did this to us?"

"I have no idea—yet."

"Story I heard is Bella figured it was one guy."

"That's what we've got."

"That's crazy," Nathan said. "He has to be good if he took out the whole crew. Hey, what about Newark? Don't we have a shipment being handled there as we speak? Another order for Poliokof? Is he still pissed because he didn't get his weapons on time?"

"Poliokof isn't our only deal. That freakin' Russian needs to cool down. The world doesn't spin on his say-so. A few machine guns are late and he blows his top. But Bella didn't help matters by getting all mouthy with him."

"What's this I hear about Bertolli vanishing from his office?"

Cameron shrugged. "Yeah, that's weird. I have people looking for him."

"You did make Costanza realize he needs to stay sharp?"

Lou nodded. "He already knows to step up security."

"It'd be a good move to do the same here. Tighten up. Maybe have a word with Torrance, as well."

"Our good local sheriff is on his way right now."

"Make him remember we aren't paying him just to sit on his bony ass."

"He already knows that," Lou said.

"Make him remember even harder."

Lou smiled. "Okay, just quit playing hardball with me."

"I have to keep up my tough-guy image," Nathan said.

"Yeah, yeah, you want to play nice for that lady deputy of Torrance's. I know. You go all goofy every time you see her."

"That's not true, Lou."

"It is so. Hey, you think she's soft on you?"

Nathan shrugged.

"Not so *little* bro anymore," Cameron said.

Changing the subject, Nathan said, "I saw Tony when I came in. He was looking happy."

"I put him in charge of Chicago. Bella is out permanently."

"I know what that means."

"Yeah? So behave when I'm around."

Nathan smiled. "Hey, what about the thing in Miami? Is it connected?"

"I don't know. We're still checking it out."

"Lou, there's something weird going on. Some guy comes out of nowhere and takes down Soames's deal, then Chicago gets bounced. We lost merchandise. People are dead. There's just too much not to be connected. Listen to me, Lou."

"Take it easy," Cameron said. "I got it in hand. You think I'm not going to work this out? We are talking about our livelihood here. Look, Nate, we're not in the cuddly toy corner of the business community. The people we mix with are not exactly pillars of society. We've got to expect things like this. But we deal with it. *I'm* dealing with it."

"How did Calvera take it?"

Cameron grinned. "He was slightly pissed, but I told him he would get his shipment. Just a little late."

"Lou, are you okay? I know how things like this get to you."

"I'll be fine. But it's lucky we don't have any dogs or cats around the place. If we had they'd be running screaming with their furry butts kicked all to hell."

"Wait until we get our hands on the joker who did all this. Then you'll have something to kick."

"Yeah, you said it, bro."

5

Newark, New Jersey

Bolan entered Newark, New Jersey, off the turnpike, the GPS unit guiding him through the bustle of the late-afternoon streets to the industrial area where the auto scrap yard was based. He saw the sprawling grounds well before he reached them, a large site surrounded by corrugated iron fencing topped with razor wire. Bolan could see the stacks of wrecked vehicles rising ahead of him, the angled jibs of cranes, the sloping roof of a long workshop.

The sign on the wide-open steel gates identified the yard as South Auto Salvage.

He drove by without stopping and followed the road as it took him by other industrialized units. Bolan made a recon of the district, noting ways in and out, mapping different routes. Twenty minutes later he made the return trip and exited the area.

Okay, he thought, target spotted.

Next, he needed to carry out a recon exercise. That would be after dark. Bolan needed a base to work from. He had spotted a couple of hotels on his way in, so he backtracked and swung into the parking lot of the first one he came to. It was high end, not cheap, but that didn't worry Bolan. He was still running on his Stony Man card. He queried the man at the desk, and since there was a room available he checked in. Minutes later he was taking a long, hot shower to wash away the dust of his drive from Chicago. Room service provided a steak and salad dinner, plus fresh coffee. After his meal he stretched out on the bed and allowed himself a few hours' sleep.

Seven p.m.

BOLAN PULLED ON his blacksuit and geared up for what he hoped would be a soft probe. He took the Beretta 93-R, plus a couple of extra magazines in the pockets of his combat vest. A wire garrote, the Cold Steel Tanto knife and supple black leather gloves all went into a black backpack. He pulled on a pair of dark chinos and a roll-neck sweater. The carry-all containing his additional ordnance went to the back of the room's closet. Bolan slipped on his jacket, making sure his cell phone was there, along with a wad of cash. All for backup and the unexpected.

He left his room and took the elevator to the lobby, the backpack hanging over one shoulder. He dropped off his key card and made his way out, crossing to his car.

It took him longer to make the return journey to South Auto Salvage. Traffic was still surprisingly heavy and he drove into rain that had blown in quickly. His earlier recon had left him with a mental map of the industrial area, and he used that image to guide him to a secondary road so he could approach his target from the rear. The back strip that ran behind the scrap yard was unlit and in a state of disrepair, with dumped metal trash edging the road. Bolan pulled the rental into the shadows and cut the engine. Rain drummed on the roof. He wasn't entirely happy about leaving the car where it was, but he had little choice. There was nowhere else to park. He would have to leave it to luck that the car would still be there when he returned, or that it not be discovered at all.

Bolan removed his outer clothing. He removed combat boots from the backpack, and put them on, then donned the loaded vest and the shoulder rig for the Beretta. The Tanto was sheathed on his belt. Lastly, Bolan pulled his black baseball cap from the backpack.

He slipped from the car and locked the vehicle, pulled on his gloves and moved swiftly across the deserted strip, pressing against the corrugated iron fence surrounding the scrap yard.

The darkness worked to his advantage, his black-clad form blending in well. And the persistent rain added another plus.

Bolan walked along the rear fence from one end to the other, looking for a weak spot. He found what he was looking for close to the north corner. The corrugated sheets had been pushed into a generous outward bulge, most likely from wrecked autos being collected and pushed into stacks. He found that the overlap between two sheets had been widened, and when he moved in close he saw that the opening was large enough for him to ease through. He took his time, aware that on the other side of the fence tons of mangled steel would be balanced in close proximity to the fence. He didn't want to bring all that metal debris down on himself.

As he emerged on the far side of the fence, Bolan found himself in a narrow tunnel. Crushed cars surrounded him. On his knees, hunching his shoulders to reduce his body mass, the soldier crawled forward. The ground under him was wet and spongy, while rain worked its way down through the stacked vehicles. A couple of times Bolan was forced onto his stomach, easing his way through the close-knit formation. The soft creak of metal on metal made him pause. He waited until the creaking ceased before continuing his crawl.

Beyond his spot Bolan picked up the sound of a vehicle engine. Peering through the narrow tunnel, he found he was able to look out across the yard, past the hulks of broken vehicles. To his right was the large workshop, doors open wide and some illumination that showed him the interior. He saw figures moving about. The vehicle he had heard was new, a rain-slicked panel truck. Bolan watched as the side door opened. Two men dragged a third from inside the van. The captive had his hands bound in front of him and a hood over his head. He was hustled into the workshop, where three more figures appeared.

The prisoner started to struggle until a hard fist was slammed into his face through the hood. The guy slumped and was half-dragged when his legs gave way. Bolan watched until the group vanished from sight inside the building. Voices were competing in a lively argument, but Bolan was unable to make out any words.

He wondered about this unexpected development—he would have to get to the bottom of that later.

Remaining in position, Bolan checked out as much of the area as he could see from where he was. There were rows of stacked vehicles. Some had already been through the process that reduced them to solid, compacted blocks ready to be shipped out. The vehicle compacter was off to his left, a massive monster constructed from heavy steel and hydraulic rams. There were also heavy-duty tracked machines for moving around the wrecked vehicles. The uneven ground held oily pools of water.

Bolan mentally moved on from his visual check, turning his attention to the large workshop building. Until he knew otherwise, it would be the focus of his probe. He needed to concentrate there.

He picked up movement inside the shop, saw the group of men, minus their captive moving to the entrance. They were still engaged in some kind of heated discussion and Bolan wondered if the confrontation was about the hooded and bound newcomer. The pair from the panel truck returned to the vehicle and drove off, spinning the wheels across the greasy surface of the yard. Bolan watched the taillights gleam as the truck paused at the open gates before vanishing into the gloom beyond. He turned his attention to the three men standing just inside the workshop. One lit a cigarette, still talking to his partners. Another shrugged and raised his hands before walking back inside. The cigarette guy said something to the third man, then went inside himself. The guy left on his own stood for a moment before unzipping his thick coat. He reached inside and removed a pistol. He spent a little time checking the weapon, then jammed it back inside his coat. Even from a distance it was clear the man was unhappy.

Bolan saw this as the time to move in. He swung around the extreme edge of the workshop, positioned himself, then cut a direct line toward the lone watcher, slipping the Beretta into the shoulder holster to free both hands. The guy was leaning against the door frame, arms folded across his chest as he maintained his vigil. He didn't see or hear Bolan as the black-clad warrior made his approach. A deep-rooted sixth sense made the guy turn his head at the final moment.

Too late.

The Executioner struck hard and fast, his arms reaching out to encircle the guy's neck. Bolan pulled him in close, increasing the pressure with unrelenting force, and the man felt his air being shut off. He started to struggle, achieving nothing except to add to his dilemma. He used up what oxygen he had left, twisting and kicking as Bolan pulled him down to ground level, jamming a knee into the thug's back. It ended as quickly as it had started, with Bolan applying a final, savage twist that separated the guy's spine. He slumped, suddenly lifeless and unresisting. The Executioner let the man slide to the ground.

Slipping inside the workshop, Bolan used barrels and metal toolboxes for cover. The interior was large, the walls at each side cluttered with the debris of the work that went on inside the workshop. Fluorescent lights cast deep shadows across the workshop, and Bolan almost missed the sudden attack as a guy clad in soiled denims stepped into view, a long steel pry bar clutched in his meaty hands.

"What'd you do to Cole? You're dead, mother..." he yelled.

Bolan turned at the sound, saw the steel bar swinging at his head and ducked beneath it. The attacker steadied himself for a return swing. The soldier lunged forward, his left shoulder hitting the guy's midsection, following with a fist into his side, over his ribs. The man grunted and pulled back, both hands on the steel bar as he attempted a second swing. Bolan powered forward, given little chance to do anything else, and slammed bodily into the guy, pushing him across the workshop floor.

"Bastard," the guy roared, lashing out with the steel bar again.

The bar grazed the front of Bolan's vest as he pulled the Beretta from the shoulder rig and sideswiped his opponent across the skull. The man skidded on one knee, hauling the bar around for one more strike. But then Bolan triggered a single 9 mm Parabellum round that cored into the exposed skull just above the right ear, tunneling in to spin the guy to the floor. The steel bar dropped from his fingers and bounced against the concrete with a loud ringing sound.

"Son of a bitch shot Kyle."

The yell was followed by the stuttering crackle of autofire as Bolan dropped to a crouch, whirled, and saw an armed shooter coming at him from the far side of the shop. The soldier heard the sound of impacting slugs rattling at the wall of the shop behind him, then he was steadying the 93-R and laying down his own fire. His first shot missed. Bolan gripped the pistol in two hands, bringing the muzzle on track and hit the shooter with two close shots. The guy twisted as the 9 mm slugs lodged in his chest. The Executioner upped the muzzle and laid his third shot to the face, seeing the left side blossom red. The target screamed, triggering his SMG into the floor. He dropped to his knees, clutching hands reaching to his face a second before Bolan put his next shot between the eyes. The guy toppled backward, the back of his head torn open and bloody.

Bolan stood, turning at the eruption of sound coming from the rear of the shop.

This man burst into view, wielding an automatic shotgun, and he moved like a charging rhino. Bolan's finger had flicked the Beretta's selector to three-round burst, and he had the weapon leveled and on-target as the guy blundered into view from the door of a cramped office.

The shotgun moved in Bolan's direction.

The 93-R fired.

The guy's sweaty face vanished in an exploding mess of torn flesh and shattered bone, blood coloring the paler skin red. The shotgunner let out a harsh cry and fell back, the weapon slipping from his grasp. He struck the workbench behind him and hung there, dripping blood on the floor.

Bolan scooped up the SMG the second man had dropped and slung it.

He waited, ears tuned to pick up any suggestion of sound. He checked out the workshop. The rain drummed against the high roof over his head. The buzz of the fluorescent lights added their own noise. The tension drained, and Bolan finally moved, checking each of the men. No signs of life. He made his way to the office where the three had been gathered and looked inside. It offered nothing. It was untidy and smelled of tobacco smoke, oil and greasy food. The walls were dotted with work-related charts and invoices, plus the inevitable centerfolds of naked women. A single desk held a telephone and a computer terminal, both having seen better days. China mugs held cold coffee dregs, and the floor was littered with crushed cigarette stubs and fast-food containers. If the yard was Costanza's base for his illegal weapons; the office didn't appear to be the hub of the operation.

Bolan returned to the workshop and heard a sound that drew his attention.

It was faint.

A regular thumping, over and over. It was a few seconds before Bolan realized it was coming from somewhere beneath where he stood. He realized he was standing close to the concrete-lined inspection pit. The thirty-foot-long, five-foot-deep pit had been sunk into the workshop floor, the sides lined with lights behind toughened glass covers. Steps at one end allowed access for people working on the underside of vehicles. Current service bays would use power lifts to raise vehicles, but this workshop was most likely decades old, harking back to when such establishments weren't plagued by stringent safety protocols.

As Bolan went down the steps, the smell of absorbed lubricants became stronger. He could understand the reason why the alternative name had come into use—*grease pits*. Dirty duckboards lay on the pit floor, water and pooled oil gleaming beneath them. A blank wall faced Bolan at the end of the pit. A closer look showed it wasn't concrete, but simply a false cover decorated to resemble concrete. He checked it out and spotted the slightly recessed, thumb-sized button. Bolan pressed it and the end panel slid to one side, revealing an opening that had steps leading down. The thumping sound became louder as he stepped through and found himself in a basement room around forty square feet. He could finally see clearly because lights had come on as the door had opened.

Bolan was able to stand upright, and the first thing he saw to catch his attention was the bound figure of the man who had been off-loaded from the panel truck. He was on his knees, using a length of wood in his bound hands to bang it against a wooden crate. His hood had been removed, and Bolan saw that his face was bloody, with swollen eyes and torn lips. He was severely battered, but the bruising did nothing to hide the defiant gleam in his eyes as he stared at the black-clad, armed figure. Bolan noticed, too, that the guy's shirt was torn and bloody.

"I'm damn sure you're not one of Costanza's inbred goons," he said. "So who the hell are you?"

6

Bolan didn't speak immediately. He was exchanging the partly used magazine in the Beretta for a fresh one.

"Those guys who delivered you. Are they coming back?"

"I wasn't exactly included in their plans. All I know for sure is it was supposed to be a one-way ride."

Bolan had looked past the guy, to the far side of the basement room. He saw stacked boxes of various sizes and shapes, but they all had a look he was familiar with. There were some plain boxes, but others were in military olive-drab, stenciled. His soft probe may have gone awry, but at least he'd found the mother lode.

Costanza's weapons stash.

On the far side of the basement were plastic-wrapped blocks of white powder. Cocaine. A wooden palette held tightly bound wads of banknotes sealed in more plastic.

"Aladdin's cave," the bound man said. "This is Costanza's own little treasure trove. What we've been looking for." He sucked in a breath, again the pain from his torn lips. "Are we going to dance around this all night?" the guy said. "Who the hell are you, and will you get these damn cuffs off me?"

The guy thrust his plastic-bound wrists at Bolan.

"As far as I know *you* could be one of Costanza's dirtbags. They brought you here on some gang-related issue."

The guy shook his head. "No way," he said. "Take a look. Do I have a low forehead and a straight line of eyebrows?"

Bolan glanced at him, a faint smile edging his lips.

"Look, give me a cell and I'll have half the Newark PD swarming all over this place in thirty minutes. I'm a fucking cop, dammit. Only...I..."

"Don't have any ID?"

"Yeah. Not the brightest thing to carry when you're under-cover." The guy saw Bolan's hand move to the sheathed Tanto. "Christ, look, my name is Danny Keoh. Sergeant, Newark PD. I work the OrgCrime unit. My chief is Captain Ben Cahill. Call him to confirm, but let's find ourselves a better place to have this conversation before any of Costanza's boys return."

Bolan slid out the knife and cut the plastic cuffs. Keoh shook them free, rubbing his wrists and flexing his fingers.

"Two days they had me in those things while they worked me over."

Bolan handed him the SMG. "Think you'll be able to *work* that?"

"A comic, too. Just give me the chance." He checked the weapon. "What do I call you?"

"Cooper."

"Okay, Cooper, I suggest we get our asses out of here. Before I blew my own cover, I overheard Costanza talking to his client and arranging for pickup of that ordnance. Midnight."

Bolan looked at his watch. "Gives us four hours clear," he said.

"Costanza *could* show anytime."

Bolan crossed to the weapons stash and began going through the boxes.

"What are you looking for?" Keoh asked.

Bolan held up a couple of brick-sized blocks he had located in a sealed carton.

"C-4," he said.

"What for?" Keoh said, then stared as realization hit. "Blow it up? All this?"

Bolan had turned back to the stash and came up with a small

box that held detonators. He found a coiled roll of det cord and a compact power pack.

"You can't do this, Cooper. It's evidence. The reason I went undercover. To expose Costanza's dealings in illegal weapons."

"And it's the reason why I'm here." As Bolan spoke, he was setting up the C-4, inserting the detonator caps into the explosives, attaching the cord and trailing it across the floor as he made his way back to the basement exit. "I'm not going to allow Costanza any chance of getting his hands on those weapons." He fixed Keoh with a hard stare. "Can you guarantee your people can be here in time to stop Costanza? One-hundred-percent guarantee he won't wriggle out of this? If he turns up in the next few minutes, what are our chances of bringing in your unit before he clears the place?"

Keoh had no argument to make. He shook his head in frustration. "What can I do?"

"Get up top. Keep watch. I'm right behind you."

Bolan fed the line off the roll and made his way out of the basement, climbed from the pit and kept unrolling the det cord.

"All clear," Keoh said.

Bolan stepped out of the workshop and made his way to the cover provided by one of the yard's heavy-tracked vehicles. Keoh crouched beside him, watching as the soldier attached the det cord to the compact power pack. Bolan set the power and checked the supply. A small red light verified there was power, then he depressed the main button.

The red light flickered. Nothing happened immediately, then the night came alive with noise and flame, and the ground shook. The workshop came apart, and the air was filled with hurtling metal debris that flew in every direction. Bolan felt objects clang against the heavy metal that was shielding him and Keoh. The explosion was loud, a powerful roar that battered at their ears. Fire and smoke swept across the yard. The blast radius was strong enough to topple stacked cars and drop them to the ground like metal dominoes. Even the deadweight of the machine protecting Bolan and Keoh moved.

As the sound faded, leaving only the hungry rush of the flames consuming everything combustible, Keoh glanced at Bolan. "You expected it to be as bad as that?"

"Not really," he said, "but I think the point was made." He stood up, turning to check the spot where he had entered the yard. The stacked cars wedged against the perimeter fence had been scattered by the blast. "And the gate's open, too."

They eased by the wrecked vehicles and through the breached fence, emerging on the dark perimeter road. Bolan noticed Keoh appeared to be moving progressively slower. He turned back to the man.

"You hurting?"

Keoh nodded. "I guess they did more than I realized."

Bolan put an arm around the cop, supporting him, and took them to his waiting car. He unlocked the vehicle and helped Keoh onto the rear seat. Bolan opened the trunk and shed his combat gear. He placed the SMG the cop had carried in there, then quickly pulled his civilian clothing over his blacksuit. He got in the car, fired up the engine and drove off, clearing the area and heading for the main highway.

"You still with me, Keoh?"

"Yeah."

"I need directions to the closest hospital," Bolan stated.

Keoh pushed himself to a sitting position and looked through the window to familiarize himself with their surroundings. He was able to give Bolan the directions he needed.

"You still didn't tell me who you are, Cooper," Keoh said. "You can handle yourself, that's a given. No cops. No backup. You an Agency guy?"

"Maybe."

Keoh gave a soft chuckle. "With the way you were dressed, I could imagine black ops. You understand explosives. Ordnance. This some kind of military operation? You latched on to Costanza's main connection? The Cameron organization?"

Bolan stayed silent.

Cameron?

That name again. Something Keoh had learned from his undercover assignment?

"Cooper? Come on, man, work with me. Give me something. I'm not a complete idiot."

"There are connections between Costanza and a guy named Fredo Bella. Chicago. Same outfit. And all the way back to Miami. I've been following through."

"Yeah. I heard. Jesus, you were the one who hit all of them?"

"It needed doing. The supply of weapons to the streets is getting out of hand. Cops are being outgunned, they can't match what the gangs are buying—military hardware. Those cops in Miami were slaughtered because they couldn't take on the opposition."

"That was bad," Keoh said.

"So what did you learn about this guy Cameron?" Bolan asked.

"Costanza's boys have pretty slack security when it comes to conversation, like a bunch of old women gossiping on the front porch. This Lou Cameron works out of New Mexico. He has the illegal weapons business pretty well sewn up according to what I overheard. He buys in from his sources and ships out across the country. Bella and Costanza may have been big on their own turf, but Cameron holds the strings. He's some piece of work. I might have gotten more, but then I got made and all I learned after that was how much pain a body can take."

"Is Cameron under any kind of investigation?"

"That I can't tell you," Keoh said. "New Mexico is a long way from here. He could be on the national OrgCrime list, but what the hell, Cooper. If he's as smart as the rest, he'll be ringed by lawyers and bought help. You're into the game so you know how these lowlifes work."

"And I have the solution worked out, too."

"Like back there?"

Bolan raised his head and looked into the rearview mirror. He saw Keoh staring back at him. The cop nodded slowly. He understood.

"Hell, Cooper, *your* rules, huh?"

"Works for me."

It always had.

It always would.

Bolan's rules.

He'd bring the fight to those who sought to profit by tearing apart the rights of the innocents, the ones who were unable to fight back. Bolan, the Executioner, brought judgment to the animals who savaged their own kind for little else but profit.

Bolan's rules.

They still worked for him.

Within ten minutes the soldier was parking the car outside the hospital's emergency department. He opened the rear door and eased out the weakened, still protesting, Keoh.

"This is crazy," the cop was saying, but his strength was fading even as Bolan half carried him inside.

"This man needs help," Bolan said to the nurse at the desk. "He's been badly beaten and could have internal injuries."

The nurse called for assistance and orderlies moved into action. Bolan moved to the station and picked up a pen and a piece of paper. He wrote down his cell phone number, turned and pressed the folded paper into Keoh's hand.

"Call me if you need to."

Keoh nodded, then lay back on the gurney that had been wheeled up to the station.

"I owe you, Cooper."

The gurney was wheeled away, leaving Bolan to turn to the nurse.

"Miss," Bolan said, "listen to me. That man is a police officer. His name is Danny Keoh. You need to call Newark PD and locate a Captain Ben Cahill. He's Keoh's commander. It's important you let him know what's happened and that he gets protection here ASAP. Understand?"

The nurse nodded and moved to pick up a phone. The moment she turned away Bolan walked back outside, climbed into the car and drove off.

THE FOLLOWING MORNING Bolan was finishing his room service breakfast when his cell phone rang.

When he answered the call, he didn't recognize the voice until the speaker identified himself.

"Ben Cahill, Cooper."

"How's Keoh, Captain?"

"He's fine, thanks to you. The way things went down I guess you broke every rule in the book, but for what you did for Danny, you have the gratitude of my entire watch. This call is off the record and I'll deny it was ever made. Danny told me exactly what happened. He came close to being one dead cop before you showed up."

"Glad to be of help."

"Danny will be hospitalized for a few weeks. Those bastards worked him over bad. Broken ribs, damage to his internal organs, and he's never going to get his good looks back, but he'll survive. Now, he tells me you still didn't fill him in with who you work for, or who you really are. By the book I should have my men out looking for you. Trouble is, I don't think they'd put much effort into it."

"Thanks for that."

"Cooper, or whatever your name is, are you staying around my town for much longer?"

"No."

"No offense, but that's good news. I'd hate for some over-eager rookie to spot you and go all righteous. You understand what I mean?"

"I won't make problems for you, Captain. Not unless—"

"Cooper, I don't want to hear it. Let me just say I know, hell every police officer in the country knows by this point, about the cop killings in Miami. And the firepower these dirtbags are supplying to the gangs. Our hands are tied, Cooper."

"Not mine."

The line went quiet for a heartbeat. There was slow release of breath before Cahill said, "*Damn*. I knew I was right." His voice softened to a whisper. "Been on my mind ever since I spoke to Danny. The way he described you, blacksuit and all. Coming out of nowhere. You understand what I'm getting at?"

"I'm listening."

"I've been around a long time, Cooper. Still got a cop's memory for past things."

Bolan could see where this was leading. "Memories can play tricks."

Cahill chuckled at that. "Not these memories, son. The kind that stick. A guy in black making life hell for the perps we couldn't touch. He came and went. Had the law chasing him all over hell's backyard. Stories had it there were a lot of cops who unofficially sided with him. That mean anything, Mr. Cooper? Some say this guy died in Central Park. I'm not buying it."

"I couldn't possibly comment on that, Captain Cahill. Thanks for the heads up on Keoh. Tell him I said hello."

"One last item might interest you. Danny came up with a name. Zader Poliokof. Not much in the computers apart from the suspicion he's Russian *Mafiya*. If it's true, then we have worse problems than we figured. These guys are mean. Get involved, or cross them, and they haunt you for the rest of your life."

"Did Keoh have any other details?"

"Only that he thought Poliokof was the buyer for the weapons they had stored at the scrap yard. Costanza has a banker who handles all his cash transactions. He works out of a dry-cleaning shop." Cahill quoted the address for Bolan. "The guy who runs it is Manny Gottfried. I add that last item purely for your interest, Cooper."

The call was terminated and Bolan stared at the cell phone, shaking his head at the contact that had come from out of left field. Unexpected, enlightening, and it would allow him a final pass at Costanza's setup before he left town.

7

Zader Poliokof had ambition. Too much, perhaps, because his desire to become even more powerful than he already was often took him into uncharted and dangerous waters. Despite this he was never afraid to take chances. And so far his gambles had always paid off in the end. His understanding of life lay in the simple premise that if you never took a risk you would never advance. And as far as Poliokof was concerned, "advance" meant strengthening your grip on whatever was around you.

The failure of the Costanza deal had planted the seed in Poliokof's mind. His Russian Mafiya Family was always looking for ways to expand. New merchandise. Fresh fields. Spreading the influence of the organization. Poliokof already had a viselike grip over the territory under his control. He'd already begun looking beyond the local area. Through his direct and indirect network of informants he had learned about Costanza's and Bella's problems. He rephrased that thought. Bella no longer had problems. He had been found dead in his Chicago hospital bed, and from what Poliokof had heard, the man had not died from the injuries that put him there. One less thing to concern himself with.

Poliokof's anger over the way Bella had reacted to Leminov over the failure to deliver on the Miami deal had only been inflamed by the total loss of the large consignment here in Newark. Someone was inflicting heavy damage on the

Cameron organization. Beyond the destruction of his weapons order, Poliokof didn't care about Cameron's troubles. He had to sort that himself. And while he was involved in that, Poliokof would use the distraction to launch his own attack on the business.

So that brought him to Nicky Costanza, the local capo. The man was nothing but a low-level hood. He had no class. He was, as far as Poliokof was concerned, inferior. The way his base had been attacked and destroyed simply showed he didn't have the skill to even protect himself. Poliokof saw the strike against Costanza as an opportunity to step in and make his bid for the Cameron franchise.

No one had any idea yet who was behind the disastrous strike against Bella and Costanza. The only description they had was sketchy at best.

A single man.

Clad all in black.

Well-armed and ruthlessly efficient.

He had moved in, taken down his targets and was gone before any kind of response could be actioned.

The single, most obvious question that needed answering was why the guy also destroyed the weapons. Thousands of dollars' worth of new, state-of-the-art ordnance, reduced to blackened and twisted pieces of metal. It was a puzzle Poliokof had not yet been able to solve.

Someone had targeted the Cameron bases, killed his people, then destroyed the caches of weapons. It made little sense. Unless the hitter was some kind of vigilante who had a simple agenda—to make Cameron hurt on all counts. Poliokof found that hard to accept. He knew it wasn't an impossibility but he saw it as vague.

Whoever the mystery man was, he had done Poliokof a favor. By striking at Cameron's Chicago and Newark operations he had opened the way. Poliokof had been casting his eyes toward the South for some time, aware of the potential in Cameron's business. The need for firepower came from numerous sources. America was awash with weapons; they simply needed channeling in the right direction. From street gangs to drug peddlers fighting to maintain their hold on the market, to crime syndicates and the antigovernment militia groups stockpiling their canned food and guns for Armageddon out in the badlands—guns were part of America's culture. Poliokof had seen this as a big money earner. Being the head of his Russian *Mafiya* crew, he already had insider knowledge. He knew the customer base and how to expand it on a large scale. Only in America could a man outside society make his fortune by supplying weaponry to the rest of the criminal fraternity.

No, he thought, returning to his original idea, expansion was helped when the opposition was unsure of his own position, when unexpected events upset the usual routine. Lou Cameron would be wondering just what the hell was going on. Now was the time for Poliokof to make a move, to take advantage of the other man's confusion.

One thing Poliokof had learned since coming to America was that men like Cameron were tough and ruthless, but they were no match for the Russian Mob. The Russians hit harder than anyone else. Their methods were cold, instant and they acted without remorse. Their dogged persistence and the sinister way they exacted vengeance was far beyond anything the Americans could match. There were no compromises, no holding back, no second chances, and there was no limit as to what they would do to get what they wanted.

Nicky Costanza was going to be the first to experience the hell that was the Russian Mob. It would be an example for Cameron to witness.

8

Nicky Costanza was more than irritated when he showed up at Manny Gottfried's dry-cleaning business. His phone had been ringing all day, and the pressing weight of the previous night's hit had him jumping each time the shrill sound interrupted him. Gottfried's telephone call had been unexpected. The man was uncharacteristically monosyllabic. But his insistence that Costanza come to the store had sounded urgent. All Gottfried would say was that there was a big monetary problem, something that needed Costanza's appraisal and it had to be sooner rather than later. Costanza had been unable to get anything more out of the man, Gottfried saying he couldn't go into too much detail over the phone. By the time the short call finished, Gottfried was almost sobbing.

"The store will be closed," he managed to say. "Come straight up to my office."

With his two bodyguards flanking him, Costanza pushed through the store door, walked around to the rear and up the stairs. He slammed his way into the office, where Gottfried was seated in his chair behind the desk.

"So, what the hell is so important you drag me all the way over here? I got enough to deal with after what happened at the yard."

The first thing Costanza noticed was the sweat beading Gottfried's pale face and the way his eyes were flicking back and forth. Alarm bells sounded in his head, but the warning was already redundant.

Armed figures moved into view from the corners of the office flanking the door. They had raised SMGs that covered Costanza and his pair of bodyguards before any of them could reach for their weapons.

"If you feel you can shoot your way out of this…" the closer man said. He had a shark's smile on his lips. His eyes were flat, dead, with no flicker of an expression. His accent was Russian. He was tall, his body poised and muscular, his head shaved. He wore an expensive suit and shoes that had probably cost as much as Costanza's entire wardrobe.

Costanza knew him instantly. This was the first time he had come face-to-face with the man, but he knew who he was.

Zader Poliokof.

Russian *Mafiya*.

The man who had been expecting the missing weapons.

A cold roll of fear twisted in Costanza's stomach.

As if he understood how Costanza was feeling, Poliokof gestured toward the chair facing Gottfried's desk. Costanza sat down.

Poliokof nodded at his pair of bodyguards as they finished disarming Costanza's own men. Their hands were bound tightly behind them. At Poliokof's sharp command, one of his men opened the door and took Costanza's men out of the office, closing the door behind him.

"Don't glare at Manny," Poliokof said. "He had no choice when it came to calling you. He had a gun to his head at the time. It's amazing how quickly loyalty goes out the window when the choice is limited. Manny did not want his brains blown out through the back of his skull." Poliokof raised the heavy black pistol in his hand. It did not escape Costanza's notice that the weapon had a suppressor attached to the muzzle. "Unfortunately the threat was only suspended temporarily. Once Manny called you it was restored." He glanced across at Gottfried. "I forgot to tell you, Manny."

Poliokof leveled the pistol and fired twice, the slugs coring in just above Gottfried's left eye. His head snapped back under the impact, one of the slugs burning its way through to blow out the back of his skull, depositing bloody gore on the leather headrest of the seat as it lodged in the frame. The chair rolled back a few inches, swaying slowly as Gottfried slumped.

"Tell me, Nicky, have you been trying to avoid me?" Poliokof, not known for his tolerance or forgiveness, raised a hand and his remaining bodyguard closed the office door. "I wouldn't look at it favorably if I thought you were playing games."

Costanza forced a conciliatory smile. "Hey, we're in the middle of a deal. Why would I want to skip out?"

"Then where are my guns? I don't see my guns. You were contracted to supply me. Oh, I remember. You lost the Miami consignment, and the ones here in Newark sort of got blown up."

"A slight logistics problem. It's being sorted out even as we speak," Costanza said in a casual, too slick way.

"*Logistics?* So is that what it is called now?" Poliokof spoke in Russian to his man. It raised a laugh.

He turned again to Costanza. "Do not treat me like an idiot, Nicky. I know what is going on. Your fucking employer is in bad trouble. Two hits already. Miami and Chicago. And now a third here in Newark. My consignment has been destroyed. Blown all over the landscape. There is no *logistical* problem. You took my money, and my guns have been destroyed. I want what is mine, and I want it now. If I can't, then you have to absorb the cost. And if you can't, then I will take it out of Cameron's hide."

Costanza was aware of the reputation of the various Russian Mobs. They had zero tolerance when it came to exacting satisfaction. Talk was useless, because people like Poliokof didn't listen to excuses. There was never a compromise with them. That would imply weakness on their part, something they could not tolerate. It was strength through intimidation. By never giving an inch, the Russians maintained absolute control. Costanza sensed the slow movement of Zader's bodyguards.

The one who had left with Costanza's men had come back into the office. The pair moved across the room to stand on either side of him. He realized he was in deep trouble.

"Mr. Poliokof, give me the chance to make this right. I'm sure I can work out something to your satisfaction."

"You obviously don't understand my position, Nicky. Letting me down means you have also let down my organization. We do not accept failure. If this gets out, it shows us in a bad light. Others will see and think they can treat us casually. As a businessman you must see the impossibility of letting this happen. Show weakness and the hungry dogs will go for your throat." Poliokof stroked a hand across his smooth, shaved skull. "Understand, Nicky, this is purely a business decision. I'm sure you have heard the phrase 'it's not personal.' Well, now you can experience it yourself."

"For Christ's sake, Zader, this doesn't have to happen."

Poliokof took a step back.

A swift movement alerted Costanza to the two bodyguards moving in. He tried to push up out of his seat, but powerful hands clamped down on his wrists, pinning them to the arms of the chair. Costanza stared up into the cold, hard features of the burly man holding his arms immobile. His panicked thoughts reminded him there were two of them. Where was the second guy? He received his answer in the form of a cold, thin length of wire that was snapped around his neck.

Costanza felt the wire pull taut, sinking deep into his flesh. He tried to scream, but the garrote was already cutting into his neck, shutting off his ability to yell. Cold, slithering fear engulfed him. He struggled in vain, not realizing his actions were only helping to increase the effect. Costanza didn't care. He wanted the cruel grip of the wire to end. He was left thrashing and kicking, only increasing his advancing death. Blood bubbled up from the where the garrote had sliced into his flesh. The bodyguard holding his wrists let go and stepped back, watching Costanza impassionately, stepping to one side so he wasn't blocking Poliokof's view. Costanza reached up and clawed at his bloody throat. His fingers were unable to touch the wire now sunk deep into his throat. All he could do was writhe and jerk, half off the seat now, his body weight dragging the wire deeper. He gasped and flailed. His tongue protruded from his bloody, slack mouth. Costanza's heels drummed on the floor, leaving dark streaks on the boards.

The light was starting to fade as he sank into oblivion. Costanza flopped on the loop of wire, not even aware he had wet the front of his pants as his control went. His killer gave a final tug on the wire, then released his grip and Costanza's flaccid body slumped to the floor. He half rolled onto his side, his left arm making spasmodic movements for a few seconds.

Poliokof stared down at the corpse. He prodded it with the toe of one expensive shoe, as if convincing himself Costanza was really dead. He bent and felt through the dead man's pockets until he found his cell phone. He proceeded to take a number of photographs of Costanza and Gottfried. He checked Costanza's contact list, found the number for Cameron and sent the photos to the man.

Satisfied, he gestured for his men to leave. Following them out, and said, "Tell the boys downstairs in the parking garage to stay around in case any of Costanza's people show up. If they do, they can join their former employer. It will increase the pressure on Cameron. And he won't be happy when he receives the pictures I took."

9

Bolan parked across the street from the dry-cleaning store. It was late afternoon. Dark clouds hung low over the city, and rain was starting to wet the streets. He would visit Manny Gottfried and conclude his business before he vacated Newark.

He had contacted Jack Grimaldi earlier in the day to arrange a pickup once he'd completed his deeds in New Jersey.

"Jack, are you free? I need a lift somewhere." Bolan asked when the Stony Man pilot answered his call.

"When, buddy?"

"Now," Bolan stated.

"Tell me where you are and I'll warm up the bird."

"You sure you can do this? I don't want to take you away from other business."

"No problem. I'm between missions at the moment—lucky for you."

Bolan laid out his needs and Grimaldi listened.

"No involvement for you apart from the ride."

"If you say so, Sarge. But you know I'm here if you change your mind," Grimaldi said. "It'll take me around five hours to reach you. I know a small private strip in your neck of the woods, so you be there and we're a go. I'll give you a call when I hit base."

GOTTFRIED'S DRY-CLEANING business sat between a fast-food outlet and a used-book store. At one corner of the building Bolan saw the exit for the multilevel parking garage. The way into the garage was at the opposite end. He looked the building over. Whatever it might have been in the past, the place had a decidedly down-market look to it. On the floors above the dry-cleaning business many of the windows were dark, in some instances blacked out.

It was the kind of setup a man like Costanza would use for his cash drop-off point. Over the years Bolan had come to recognize this almost classic cover, a quiet, outwardly respectable business that effectively provided cover for illegal transactions. It was a front to conceal the hub of a profitable backroom enterprise. It went back to the old Prohibition days of the Al Capone empire, when outwardly honest stores were used to hide crooked dealings. A simple, but workable ploy—hiding in plain sight.

Behind the drab frontage, Gottfried would take in cash from Costanza's transactions and work his sleight of hand to make it disappear. Money laundering—and Bolan was not slow in seeing the irony of using a dry-cleaning business as a front— was a process criminal organizations employed universally to manipulate large sums and ease them into the financial system. Passed around, through shell companies, transferred and eventually brought back as clean money, it was part of the criminal machinery. If nothing else, organized crime employed a great deal of ingenuity when it came to protecting its illegal profits.

Bolan understood the frustration of cops like Danny Keoh and Captain Cahill. Despite their dedication and personal risk, the effort they put into a case against the Costanzas of the criminal world, there was little they could do unless evidence was irrefutable and all the legalities had been covered. Months of input could be dismissed if a single word was out of place. Bolan's sympathy was with the cops. They might know an individual was guilty, but were powerless if they made a single, simple misstep.

Which was why Bolan stepped in to correct those anomalies.

His intervention at least cleared the way for the beleaguered cops, gave them hope to carry on with their lawful work with the knowledge someone was doing something to combat evil in its purest form.

Bolan was about to enter the dragon's den, to face whatever awaited him. In his world any confrontation tended to veer to the hostile. He touched the 93-R nestling in its holster beneath his jacket. His Tanto knife was sheathed against his left hip, pushed to the back of his belt. He was ready both physically and mentally for whatever he found.

Bolan started his engine and eased the vehicle into traffic, taking the first turn he came to. He drove until he spotted a quiet alley between buildings, rolled to a stop, cut the engine and stepped out of the vehicle. He locked the rental, turned and walked back to Gottfried's building. As he crossed the street he saw the Closed sign on the store's door. He turned and made his way to the parking-garage entrance and slipped inside. There was no booth. No barrier. The interior was poorly lit, most of the ceiling lights nonfunctioning. He could hear water dripping somewhere close by. Only a couple of vehicles were in view. On an impulse Bolan checked them out, especially intrigued by an expensive-looking SUV. It was a high-end vehicle, and it looked out of place in the gloomy garage. The soldier passed a hand over the hood, feeling the heat from an engine recently turned off. When he checked the interior, he noted the expensive, soft leather upholstery and the abundant electronics.

He made his way to the door, pushing through and checking out the corridor. Empty. The decor had long since lost its shine. The carpet underfoot was worn, the color faded. To Bolan's left, stairs led to the next floor. He unbuttoned his jacket so he could access the Beretta.

A trace of unease uncoiled itself as he moved along the corridor. The silence was unnatural. The soldier was sure he was not alone—he sensed a closeness, a presence.

Bolan drew the Beretta and moved the selector switch to three-round burst. He held the weapon at his side, the barrel in-line with his thigh.

The first door he came to had Gottfried's name on it. He tried the handle, and the door opened to his touch. Bolan looked inside. Across from him was the main door, and display window, a counter and racks holding clothing in transparent covers waiting for collection.

A shadow slipped out from behind one of the racks, crossing the floor, coming at Bolan. The slim blade of the knife in his left hand caught the light as it was thrust at its intended target. Bolan saw a hard, bony face, cold eyes. No sound. No hesitation in the guy's moves. Just the driving force that sped him in for the kill.

That never happened.

The unseen pistol in Bolan's hand came into play with hard-edged precision. The would-be assassin was no more than three feet from Bolan when the Beretta's muzzle centered on his face. An expression of pure shock crossed the guy's face in the brief instant before the 93-R's subsonic 9 mm slugs caved it in. The three-round burst at close range collapsed the face and turned it into a bloody ruin. One of the mangled slugs cored all the way through and blew out the back of the man's skull, leaving a mess of bone and brain fragments behind. He slumped to the floor, his body in spasm.

Bolan returned to the corridor, searching for the door that would take him through to the rear of the building and the heart of the dry-cleaning operation. Farther along he saw a pair of wide rubber doors. As he reached them, he picked up the odors of the chemicals used in the cleaning process. He peered through the transparent windows set in the upper section of the doors. His guess had been correct. Through the doors was the cleaning system, with its equipment and machinery. A winding overhead track held clothing suspended for transport. But the track was still now and the mass of machinery covering the area was silent.

Bolan crouched and eased his way through the doors, keeping to one side as he entered the process area.

No sound. No movement. Bolan proceeded with caution. He

had thought the front of the shop had been deserted. He wasn't about to make that assumption again.

He checked out the area, not moving until he was satisfied it was clear.

Two more doors stood at the far side. One was a metal roller door that would take him to the access area outside. The other was in the side wall. Bolan crossed to it in a series of quick moves, using as much cover as he could. The door stood slightly open, and through the gap the soldier saw stairs leading to the next floor. He edged the door open with the barrel of his Beretta until it touched the wall on the other side, then went through. The Executioner went up the stairs and reached the landing. To his left was a door marked Parking Garage. The door to his right was marked Storage. From the landing another flight of stairs led to another story. At the head, a door indicated access to the garage.

The door on his right, this time, led to a short corridor with a number of doors. Bolan scanned the hall. It was clear. He moved along the corridor until he reached the office marked M. Gottfried—Private.

Bolan eased up to the door and listened for a moment. Again only silence. He turned the handle and pushed the door open.

The office was silent.

Without movement.

But it was not unoccupied.

Death made its presence known in a scene of bloody slaughter that made even Bolan step back as he took it in.

Two bodies. One was seated in the high-backed executive chair behind a cluttered desk, dead from the twin bullet holes directly over the left eye.

The second man had not been allowed to die so easily. He was slumped on the floor. There was a lot of blood down his front from the garrote that had been used to kill him. The wire was still in place, having been drawn so deeply into the soft flesh that it had severed the main artery. Before the men had bled out, a great deal of blood had pumped from his neck. It had soaked his expensive shirt and suit. It was a violent way to die.

Bolan crouched beside the body and eased open the jacket, feeling for a wallet in the man's pocket. He withdrew it, opened it and found a driver's license.

The photo and description identified the man as Nicholas Costanza. Bolan glanced across at the other man. Manny Gottfried? He checked inside the guy's coat and found a second wallet. The contents proved his guess had been correct.

Bolan stepped away from the bodies, trying to figure out what had happened.

And why.

What had he walked in on?

The killings were not random. They had been deliberate, and Bolan sensed a professional hand in the deaths. He had no doubts that Costanza would have enemies, rivals. The only question was *who* were they and why had they chosen this time to make a hit?

10

Bolan's deliberations were interrupted as he picked up on voices outside the office. He moved so he could peer around the frame and saw three armed, suited men standing at the head of the stairs leading to the lower floor. They were debating something that was also holding them back from approaching the office. He figured they had found the dead guy downstairs.

To Bolan's right was the door that led to the parking garage. It was the only way open to his escape.

Aware that the three men might push caution aside and head for the office, Bolan acted. He eased the door wide enough to get through, raised the Beretta and powered into the corridor. He fired off two three-round bursts in the general direction of the group, heard the startled yells. Return shots were fired in haste, gouging the wall, sending plaster dust across the corridor. Bolan kept moving, committed to his action. He reached the door and shouldered it open. A final shot from his pursuers thudded into the door frame inches from his head. The soldier slammed the door shut, knowing his freedom would be extremely short-lived.

The thunder of boots approaching the door and the voices shouting back and forth warned Bolan his time was running out fast. They had his scent—the hounds had taken up the chase and Bolan was the prize. The only thing they should have taken notice of was that this prize had the choice of fighting back.

The Executioner would let them chase him until he caught them. He turned and ran down the flight of concrete steps to the floor below. He had noticed there was little light, only a single fluorescent tube lighting the way down. He hit the next landing, pulled back into the shadows, waiting, and let the advance runners close the gap.

Two of them skidded to a halt on the landing when they realized his footsteps could no longer be heard. They looked around. One moved to the door, pulled it open and checked out the parking area beyond, probing with his pistol.

The guy said something over his shoulder. It was in Russian.

There was no answer from his partner. The speaker turned, his handgun probing the shadows on the landing.

"Yorgi..."

Then he saw his partner curled up on the floor about three feet away. Yorgi was hugging his throat, making low, wet mewling sounds. A spreading black pool, glistening, was edging out from under his head, and the man was barely moving.

There was a soft rush of sound and the deepest shadow close to him parted and let a shape materialize. The shape took form, a lunging man moving with speed and ease. Something slammed into his face. Pain erupted, sharp and distinctly unpleasant. He didn't have time to call out as the pain turned into a frightening numbness that engulfed his lower face. He tasted blood, felt the alien sensation of loose teeth driven from his gums, and then he was being pushed back until his lower spine was wedged against the railing that edged the landing. Powerful hands gripped his waist and upper thigh. In his fear and confusion he felt himself being lifted off his feet, tilted over the railing and his flailing hands couldn't grip anything. He fell into the open space between floors, his body bouncing from side to side as he dropped. Before he struck the floor below he had suffered a broken arm, a shattered hip and his skull was fractured in two places. He was still conscious when he hit the floor, breaking more bones and sending blood spatter across the concrete.

Bolan was on the move before the guy landed, slamming his boot against the push bar that opened the door leading to the parking garage. The Tanto was back in its sheath, the blade still bloody from slicing across Yorgi's throat. It was the Beretta's turn, the muzzle probing ahead of him, to the sides, as he moved toward the ramp. He was not out of danger yet, but this was preferable to being caught between however many gunners were behind him and others who might come at him from the garage ramp.

Shots sounded, slugs blasting powdered concrete from the side walls. Bolan kept moving until he could see the darting shapes flitting in and out of the crisscrossed shadows. He rounded the curve in the ramp, saw an armed guy scrambling over the adjoining wall to get a clear shot. The guy had allowed his gun hand to stray off-line as he made the jump. Bolan paused, bringing up the 93-R. He triggered a triburst and saw the guy lose balance and drop.

Ahead of Bolan two more armed figures came charging up the ramp, weapons firing, the autofire falling short. They hadn't compensated for the angle of the slope, or for the fact that they were on the move, arms jerking erratically. Bolan gave them no chance to correct the error. He held the Beretta in a two-handed grip and tracked his targets, putting them down with three-round bursts. As he walked on, passing the sprawled figures, they were bleeding out over the scuffed, oily concrete.

Bolan waited, crouched, his eyes moving back and forth. There were no more shots, no advancing figures from behind, or moving up the ramp. He remained where he was until his senses told him all of his attackers were down. They had expected him to be an easy target—they had been wrong and had paid the price. He moved, still cautious, making his way to the street-level exit. At the exit Bolan hugged the shadows, checking the street beyond the building. Streetlights cast pale light on the wet sidewalk. There was no movement, no sign of further opposition.

Bolan put away the Beretta and zipped his jacket, turning up the collar against the rainy and chill Newark evening. He cut across the street and retraced his steps to where he had left his rental.

Inside the car he took out his cell phone and speed-dialed Captain Ben Cahill.

"I picked up your suggestion," Bolan said, "and paid a call to Manny Gottfried's place."

"Any joy?"

"I'd hardly call it that," Bolan said. "Someone beat me to it. Gottfried was dead in his chair. Two bullets in his head. Something else, too. His boss, Costanza, was there, as well. He had a garrote wrapped around his throat. It cut deep enough to sever his arteries."

"Jesus," Cahill whispered.

"Whoever did the killing left a cleanup team behind to deal with any stragglers."

"You cause any damage?"

"They gave me no alternative," Bolan said. "Cahill, they spoke Russian. What does that tell you?"

The cop didn't say anything for a couple of beats. "I'm thinking Russian *Mafiya*. Main guy around the district is Zader Poliokof, a mean son of a bitch. He'd as soon cut off your hand than shake it."

"Maybe when you check out the dead you might recognize them. The Russian Mob usually has specialized tattoos that should tell you their affiliation. If they are Poliokof's crew, it looks like there's an organized crime fallout brewing."

"Poliokof has been looking for a chance to expand. Your business in town has likely set him in motion." Cahill cleared his throat. "Cooper, I am damn glad you're moving on. Much as I understand your motivation, I figure you've filled your quota here. You get the hell out of Newark and let me deal with the mess."

"I'm done here, Captain. I'll be gone in the next couple of hours."

"See to it that you are, and try to stay clear of my town for a while."

Bolan cut the call. He started the car and eased out of the

alley, heading back to his hotel. He needed to pick up his belongings and check out before he drove to make his rendez-vous with Grimaldi.

His upcoming trek to New Mexico would take him far from Newark's chill and rain. In its place would be the dusty environs of the Southwest, an open landscape under cloudless skies.

Bolan already had a feeling he was going to find plenty of heat there—and not all of it down to the climate.

11

"You like it hot, Sarge? Well, you sure as hell got it," Grimaldi said.

The Gulfstream C-21A had touched down at the small strip, the Stony Man pilot cruising across the concrete apron to come to stop alongside a couple of aircraft parked outside a hangar. Next to the building a tacked-on office displayed the name Sandro Air.

"I get the feeling you know the owner," Bolan said, preparing to off-load his gear.

"Sandro and me, well, we hang out whenever I'm in the area," Grimaldi said.

A slim figure dressed in dark blue coveralls and a baseball cap sauntered out of the office and came to meet Grimaldi. Bolan smiled when he saw the attractive young woman. She threw her arms around the pilot and kissed him openly and without embarrassment. Grimaldi returned the embrace.

Bolan stood to one side until the pair decided they had exhausted the greeting.

"So this is how they *hang out* in New Mexico," he said.

Grimaldi grinned. "Kind of covers things," he said. "This is Melina Sandro. Mel, a good buddy of mine. Matt Cooper."

The soldier returned the firm handshake. The young woman was beautiful, with dark hair and a lightly tanned skin. Her eyes were large, brilliantly violet and her generous mouth showed even, white teeth. Bolan could understand why his friend liked her.

"Good to know you, Coop," she said. "How do you know this sky bum?"

"Long story," Bolan said.

Her grin was as bright as her eyes.

"You boys ready for some of my famous coffee?"

"It's the only reason I ever come here," Grimaldi said.

In the snug, tidy office Sandro poured them mugs of her hot, rich brew. Bolan had to admit it was good.

"So what brings you down here?" the woman asked.

"Business."

She obviously sensed there was more to the story, but Bolan gave her credit for not probing.

"Jack, are you going to be around for a while?" she asked him.

"Until Cooper is ready to leave," Grimaldi said, eyeing Bolan.

The office phone rang and Sandro moved to answer it,

"I'll keep the home fires burning," Grimaldi said. "I'll wait here until you call for a ride out." He nodded in Sandro's direction. "I have plenty to keep me busy, Sarge."

"I need transport," Bolan said.

"Well, it's twelve miles to Las Cruces. I can borrow a truck from Melina and drive you there. You can have your pick of rental agencies and be on your way."

"Let's do it. I need to move on this before I lose momentum."

BOLAN CHECKED into the isolated motel he'd spotted as he cruised the highway leading to McQueen. He had decided to rest before making the final run to the town. In the morning he would resume his journey and reach his target location by midday. He parked his dusty SUV and hauled his gear into the room, locking the door.

After renting the SUV in Las Cruces and saying goodbye to Grimaldi, Bolan had spent time making some purchases.

He had used some of the cash he had acquired from the arms deal in Miami and had bought camera equipment, moving from store to store so he didn't make a large purchase in one place that might arouse suspicion. When he drove out of Las Cruces, he had his assorted photographic gear on the rear seat.

His cover story would have him as a freelance photographer working up material for a proposed article. It wasn't the most original idea but it would, hopefully, allow him to move around the county at will while he made his recon. He needed time to check out Cameron and his organization and formulate a plan of attack.

Bolan understood and accepted that no matter how meticulous a plan might seem, there was always the human element to consider. He knew that no amount of effort could cover unseen factors.

CAMERON OIL MAINTAINED an office in town. It was situated on Main Street, across from the café where Bolan was having his meal. During the time he sat idly watching through the window, the office had a couple of visitors. One was just a delivery guy, but the second drew Bolan's attention—a young man, well dressed, who walked with a limp. He pulled up outside the office and climbed out of a bright red Ferrari. He stopped to talk with a uniformed deputy from the town sheriff's department. The deputy, clad in tan shirt and pants, was overweight, his soft stomach straining his shirtfront. The two men appeared to be extremely friendly.

The café waitress, a friendly woman with a badge on her blouse that read Cora, poured Bolan a refill and noticed him looking across the street. When he'd come into the café, Cora had observed he was new in town and Bolan had used the opportunity to explain his presence, showing her the camera he carried with him.

"This is a small town," Cora had said. "A new face is hard to miss. We don't get many visitors, being way off the interstate. Apart from tourists in the summer, that is. It gets dull sometimes, but it's how folks like it. Me, well, I love to meet a fresh face." She had placed his meal in front of him. "Enjoy, honey."

Now she said, "If you're thinking of adding him as one of your subjects, forget it. He's a mean one. I'm damn sure he blames the world for his bad leg. He's liable to run you over with that fancy car of his if you tried to take his picture."

"Thanks for the warning. I don't want to bother anyone. Is he a local celebrity or something?"

Cora laughed. "Nathan Cameron a celebrity? He might figure he's somebody special. He just walks in his big brother's shadow."

"Brother?"

"Lou Cameron. He owns Cameron Oil, which refines and transports oil for a number of local outfits. His place is about twenty miles south of town." She finished topping up his coffee. "Word of advice, honey—wipe Cameron Oil off your list, as well. It's not what I'd call a people friendly company."

"That sounds like good advice, Cora. I just want some nice pictures. No aggravation."

He didn't let her know that Cameron Oil and its owners were just what he had come to town for. Cora's information would be added to what Bolan already had for the upcoming recon.

So far he knew that the oil company was isolated and visitors weren't welcome. Barrels of oil and a transport division didn't exactly warrant unsociability—unless Cameron Oil had more on its books than it was owning up to.

Bolan drank his coffee, his mind winding ahead to what he had to do. Going on his intel, it was looking more and more likely that Cameron's desert enterprise *was* the central base of his operation. All Bolan needed was confirmation. And if he got that incriminating evidence, then the Cameron site was going to be on the receiving end of a Bolan Blitz. He would hit the refinery and reduce it to ashes—the Cameron brothers along with it.

The Executioner was going to put the company out of business and retire its owners permanently.

12

The single-lane road out of McQueen ran in a straight line through semiarid terrain. Cactus, scrub, sand and the hot sun surrounded Bolan. He drove at a steady speed, not wanting to exceed the speed limit. He didn't need the local law pulling him over.

His GPS was showing he was no more than a mile from the turnoff that would lead him to Cameron Oil. Bolan eased off the gas, letting the SUV slow. According to the screen readout, the side road was still a county road, not a restricted private one, so there was nothing to prevent Bolan from using it.

The shrill, undulating sound of a siren caught his attention. Bolan checked his rearview mirror and saw a large black-and-white SUV police vehicle coming up behind him. He dropped his speed and pulled across to the dusty shoulder. Bolan cut the engine and sat waiting patiently as the police truck stopped. The driver's door opened, and the soldier was not at all surprised when the overweight deputy he had seen talking to Nathan Cameron climbed out. The guy moved slowly, right hand on the butt of his holstered pistol.

This is interesting, Bolan thought. He had only been in town a few hours and the local cops were showing an interest in him already. He sat back, window powered down and both hands on the steering wheel, and waited for the deputy to reach him.

"I want to see your…" The guy stopped when he realized

Bolan's hands were in plain sight. He maintained his belligerent expression, and his gun hand stayed exactly where it was. He took a breath. Sweat glistened on his soft face and he blinked away where it had run into his eyes.

"Is there a problem, Deputy?" Bolan asked quietly as he handed over his driver's license.

"I'll decide that. You just stay still."

Bolan decided to let the deputy do his job. His passive attitude had already thrown the guy off his stride.

The name tag on the man's strained shirt read Magruder. He handed back Bolan's license and stepped away from the side of the SUV, his eyes searching the interior, front and back.

"What's in the bags?"

"My equipment."

"Such as?"

"Photographic gear. Cameras, flash units. I'm a photographer."

"Show me," he demanded, the gun hand gripping the pistol butt tightly.

"Can I move, Deputy? You did say to stay still."

"One thing I can't stand is a smart mouth."

"Just doing what I was told."

Magruder moved well clear of the vehicle, pulling his pistol and aiming it at Bolan. "Out of the vehicle, you son of a bitch. Don't try smart-mouthing me, boy, 'cause you picked the wrong man to do it to."

Bolan opened his door and stepped out, keeping both his arms well away from his body as he waited for Magruder's next move. As setups went, this one was so clumsy it might have been laughable under different circumstances.

"Show me what's in those bags. Lift them out of the car and place them on the ground. You do it slow, boy, and don't give me a reason to shoot you."

"I'm surprised you need one, Deputy Magruder. Is this the way you treat all visitors to the county? Now, unless you can give me a valid excuse for wanting to pry into my personal belongings I'm not taking those bags out of the vehicle. You've already given me enough to call my lawyer in Los Angeles, and when I tell him what's happened here, your sheriff is going to be wondering what hit him."

"Don't fuck with me, boy," Magruder said. Bolan sensed a lowering in his aggressive attitude.

"I was driving well below the limit, on a county road. I stopped when you signaled me, offered no resistance and did what you said. So what are you charging me with, Deputy Magruder? Just so I can inform my legal adviser, you understand."

"I could cuff you right this instant and haul your ass to jail."

"You could," Bolan said. "Sooner or later I would still get my phone call and then the trouble starts. For you, I mean." He watched the sweat run from beneath the brim of Magruder's hat. "It's hot out here, Deputy. Maybe we should drive back to town and I'll have a face-to-face with your sheriff and we can sort this out."

"The hell we will," Magruder replied. "I got cause to hold you."

"Oh? Better read me my rights and hope it sticks, Magruder, because you don't have a damn thing. Take your shot and make it a good one. It might be your last one as a deputy. If I take you to court, you'll end up out of a job and your department will be facing a harassment suit."

Magruder held his ground a while longer. He was thinking hard, knowing that Bolan had outsmarted him, given him no way to turn. As dumb as he was, Magruder realized Bolan had talked him into a no-win situation. Getting some smart lawyer on his case would push Magruder deeper into the hole he had already dug for himself.

He jammed his pistol back into the holster, his face twisted into an ugly scowl. "We'll see, boy," he said. "I promise you this isn't over. I'll see you again—under *my* rules."

He stomped away, his beefy face flushed, and climbed into his SUV. Bolan watched as Magruder hauled the big vehicle past, tires burning rubber. He stayed where he was as the county patrol vehicle sped along the road, trailing a cloud of dust in its wake. He waited because he wanted to verify something in his mind, and he received his confirmation when the patrol vehicle made a left turn onto the dirt road that led toward Cameron Oil. The long dust cloud marked Magruder's passing, still visible minutes later when Bolan climbed back into his vehicle and drove on. He rolled past the turnoff and kept driving.

13

The rage in Cameron's eyes was frightening. Lonny Magruder physically backed away from the man as he moved in. Cameron's lips were pulled in a tight line—he was restraining himself with great difficulty. When he spoke, his words were delivered in a deliberate whisper that was much more intimidating than a wild rant.

"I pay you to keep things low key, Lonny. To watch and listen, not go around playing the fucking hardman."

"I was checking this Cooper guy out, Mr. Cameron."

"For what? You said yourself he wasn't breaking any laws. Just driving. So why roust him? Let's say he is some kind of lawman. All you did was make him wonder what the hell is going on around McQueen. Maybe enough to up his interest."

"I thought—"

"That's the problem, Lonny. You were thinking. Not a smart thing to do where you're concerned." Cameron walked back to his desk and sat down. "Don't I have enough to deal with—the mess back in Chicago and Newark. People dead. Merchandise destroyed. The fucking Russians acting up." He pointed a finger at Magruder. "Get your flabby ass back to town. Stay there until you get told what to do. If you see this guy again, walk away. I don't care if he's taking a piss on main street. Understand?"

"Yes, sir, Mr. Cameron."

When the door closed behind the ashen-faced deputy,

Cameron snatched up his phone, speed dialed a number and waited. He was calling Sheriff Walter Torrance, and the moment the man came on the line Cameron told him in no uncertain terms what might happen if he didn't keep his deputy in check, relating what Magruder had done.

Torrance groaned audibly over the phone. "What can I say, Lou? The guy is a walking fuckup. My orders were to watch and listen. I'll lay it on the line for him. It won't happen again."

"It better not, Walt. This is not a good time for added problems. What about your other deputies?"

"Eddie Phillips is happy to man the office. He doesn't have much ambition and even less curiosity. He's no threat. Same with the others. Lou, they're not in the loop, so don't worry about them."

"And what about Kowalski? I'm not so sure about her. Something in the way she prowls around. Hell, Walt, she's got eyes like a hawk and doesn't miss a beat."

"One thing about her, Lou, is that she works by the book. Follows orders and knows her place. I keep on her all the time. She's a mouthy bitch, but she knows I'm boss."

"Why the hell did you ever see in her?"

"You know the story. Her old man was a cop in McQueen until he got shot on the job and had to retire. He's a well-known face around town. She's keeping up the family tradition and all that crap. The mayor made it his business to see that she got a place on the force. Good PR when election time comes around," he said. "Having a woman on the team pleases his lady voters."

"Well, don't give her time to have a social life. I don't need to have her nosing around."

Torrance chuckled. "She'll love me for upping her shifts. That damn girl thrives on work. The more I give her, the better she responds."

"Keep it that way, Walt. Try to work things out without calling too much. It's why I pay you—to keep a lid on potential problems—and extra trouble is what I don't need."

"Are things that bad?"

"Only if I don't keep on top of it." Cameron almost hung up, then said, "Keep it quiet, but watch this Cooper guy. Until we know better, stay on him without making it obvious."

"I understand. Lou, should I be looking out for more visitors? What about this Russian crew? You think they might show up in McQueen County? Actually, what if this Cooper guy is working for them?"

"We watch, we listen, Walt. Look, we can't jump on every fresh face that comes to town. Not until we know who we're dealing with. If you scare too many people, we could end up with the state police riding in and asking a lot of awkward questions."

"Okay, Lou, that makes sense."

"I'm waiting to see what the Russians are going to do. This Poliokof son of a bitch is no beginner. Back in Newark he has a bad rep, so yeah, he might decide he needs some sunshine and makes the trip. These fucking Russians want to take over the country for themselves. If he decides to visit our backyard, we'll deal with him on *our* terms. If he thinks he can do his hardman act and watch me roll over, he's in for a shock."

Cameron disconnected the call and put the phone down. He swung his chair around and stared through the window. A couple of miles from where he was seated the Cameron Oil facility was working at full capacity. The legitimate arm of the company, refining products and freighting them out, had full order books. It brought in tidy sums, and every cent of that revenue went through the books. Cameron made sure that part of the business was as lily-white as possible. He kept it separate from his core enterprise—the supply of ordnance to his country-wide clients. The arms trading was conducted from a deep bunker at one corner of the extensive site. The bunker was situated next to a building structure designated as Cameron Oil's development facility and was separate from the day-to-day activities of the business. The goods were shipped in via a select number of the big tanker rigs and kept within the steel-lined, below-ground storage. Cameron employed his own, selected crew to handle the weapons. The dealing was done discreetly, and so far there had been no problems.

Not until the past week, when the series of incidents had begun. First Florida, followed by Chicago and then Newark.

It made little sense to pin the blame on Poliokof. Okay, the Russian had made it clear *he* was blaming Cameron's lack of security for allowing the strikes to take place, but Cameron pushed that aside, concentrating on the fact that whoever was responsible had destroyed the weapons, as well as taking down Cameron's men. It was a senseless act. Removing the opposition was bad enough—but why demolish new, state-of-the-art weapons? Poliokof, whatever else he might be, needed the arms he had been going to buy. There was no sane reason to turn them into scrap metal. The same reasoning went into an explanation for the hit on the late Fredo Bella's place. The destruction of prime, expensive cargo was wanton and pointless. As a businessman, it pained Cameron to think of all that stock going to waste. He could get his hands on more, sure, but it still hurt to imagine the weapons being vandalized. And there was the bad feeling the losses created among Cameron's clients. Failure to deliver was a black mark against his credibility. And his pride. He couldn't afford to allow it to happen too many times. Customer relations were hard to foster—losing those relationships was all too easy.

On top of that, Cameron had the mystery of the perpetrator, the single, shadowy guy who seemed to come out of nowhere, create mayhem and madness, then vanish just as quickly, leaving destruction in his wake.

And death.

No witnesses remained to identify him—except Bella in Chicago. Not that Bella had survived his hospital experience. His usefulness as one of Cameron's employees had been fully terminated, an example to any others who might fall short of their responsibilities. Cameron was no better off understanding the attacker, or his agenda. More than anything it was his lack of knowledge and the feeling of frustration that angered

Cameron. If he knew who this guy was and what he ultimately wanted, then he would have something to work with.

FROM THE APARTMENT formally used by Nicky Costanza, Tony Lorenzo spoke on the phone to Cameron.

"I still can't figure Costanza's murder. Who needed to do that to him?"

"Jesus, Tony, I'll fuckin' tell you who it is. That crazy Russian Poliokof. No one else has the balls to go against me. No one else on the East Coast."

"Why him?"

"*Why?* Goddamn it, Tony, the guy is in the Russian Mob. They screwed up back home so they come here and think they own America, try to muscle in on our business. Well, it isn't happening, Tony. I don't give a damn that he's pissed because he lost his fuckin' guns and went ape shit when I didn't rush over and give him his money back. I know he's had his eye on the business for a while. Since that hard ass started knocking off our shipments, Poliokof has figured this is the time to step in and take over. Well, hell, it doesn't play that way. Tony, use the bank. Go out and hire some top muscle. I want the best, and I want them down here. If Poliokof wants a war, he can have one. Call Mitch Kassalis in Kansas. He can find us the best people. Do it immediately, Tony, and get cover for Chicago and Newark so we can show these Russian jerk-offs the way *we* play the game."

"This could get serious, Lou."

Cameron laughed harshly. "You think? Tony, it's already serious. If we don't put up a fight, Poliokof will think he can just walk in and take my chair. They upped the stakes, Tony. So we keep it going."

Since arriving in Chicago, Tony Lorenzo had been checking out every contact and sending men out onto the streets, trying to get a handle on the mysterious black-clad man. He had come back with nothing positive—no sightings, no news to put even the faintest of smiles on Cameron's face.

Lorenzo's depressing report had informed Cameron of the

deaths of Nicky Costanza and Manny Gottfried. The news was not new to Cameron. He had already received the photographs sent to his cell phone via Costanza's own phone, so he was not as shocked as he would have been if Lorenzo's news had hit him cold.

"Lou, I can organize a hit. We know where Poliokof hangs out. You want me to do it?"

"Not yet. That fuck is up to something. I want to figure it out first."

"There's something else I haven't told you. I called Newark and got it from a contact at NPD. When the cops showed up at Gottfried's place, they found more dead. Not any of our boys. It seems they were Russian, identified as being known to work for Poliokof. Five or six, our contact said."

"This gets crazier every turn," Cameron said. "Poliokof takes out two of ours, then his own men get hit. What the hell is going down, Tony?"

"Are you thinking what I am, boss? This guy who hit our bases, maybe he's going for Poliokof's boys."

"Maybe."

"So who is he? Some new age Lone Ranger? A loony vigilante?"

"Keep digging, Tony. We need to work out just what the hell is going on. I'm putting you in as top man in Newark, as well as Chicago. I need your input. Delegate so that we keep the business running, but confine your priorities to finding out who this hitter it. I'll let everyone know you're running the operations."

"Okay, boss, I'll stay on it," Lorenzo said.

"Anything you need just yell," he said, then ended the call.

Cameron took a walk outside the house, trying to clear his head. Across from the sprawling ranch-style house, a couple of his hands were busy in a corral, running a new horse on a rope as they attempted to saddle the excited animal. The horse was refusing to be saddled, bucking and jumping and defying every move the pair of hands tried. Cameron stood at the fence, losing himself in the moment and letting his thoughts drift away from his business problems.

"I like to see my employees earning their wages," he said.

The hands pulled away from the horse, wiping sweat from their faces.

"We'll be doing that, boss," one of them said. "That is one tough bronc. He'll fight us all the way down to the wire."

"It'll be worth it," his partner said. "Once that feller is tamed he'll be a damn good horse."

"Keep at it, boys," Cameron said.

He watched them working for a while longer, then turned as he heard a car approaching.

It was Nathan. He spun the gleaming Ferrari to a stop and climbed out.

"You hear what happened to Lonny?" he asked.

"I was on the phone with Torrance." He jerked a thumb in the direction of the corral. "That bronc in there has more sense in his head than Magruder."

"And he's better-looking," Nathan said. "Why did Lonny roust that guy?"

"Because he's a walking, talking idiot. He made a decision to stop the guy because he's new in town and wanted to show how smart he is. Only it backfired on him. The guy knew his rights and put Magruder on the spot."

"Lou, what if this guy is the one?"

"Then he's changed his routine. Letting himself be seen out in the open. Our hitter has kept himself under the radar so far. And coming out here is not like Chicago or Newark. Back there he could lose himself in the city. This is wide-open country, not so easy to hide in. And why let himself be spotted? This guy is a hit-and-run specialist. Nathan, I'm not saying he couldn't be our guy. That's why I'm keeping him in the spotlight. We monitor his movements. We stay sharp."

Nathan nodded. "Yeah. So, has anything happened back east?"

"I put Tony in charge of Newark, as well as Chicago. Told him to concentrate on this badass in case he's still there working on some fresh hit."

Nathan nodded. "That's good. If anyone can figure it out,

it's Tony. What about Poliokof and his goons? You going to do anything there?"

"Working on it, brother, working on it."

Just over an hour later Cameron's cell phone rang. It was Tony Lorenzo and the news he delivered this time actually brought a smile to Cameron's face.

"Boss, I think we got him," Lorenzo said. "We were out of luck on the streets, so I figured okay, maybe he moved on. I called an IT contact and had him run checks on local airports around Newark. He came up with a flight plan put in by a pilot of a private aircraft. The flight plan was for a single passenger to be flown to Las Cruces, New Mexico. The plane touched down at a small local strip, and it's still there. No return flight yet. I had my guy extend his search to rental agencies in Las Cruces. He picked out a guy renting an SUV on an open lease. The name on the rental form was Matt Cooper. The times are in line with your guy showing up in McQueen." Lorenzo gave the vehicle model and the license number. "Check it out with Torrance. See if there's a match."

"Hey, good stuff, Tony." He relayed what had happened involving Lonny Magruder. "Lonny is not going to be happy when I tell him he was possibly face-to-face with the guy."

Lorenzo laughed. "I'd like to see the look on his fat face when you do."

"I just bawled him out for stopping Cooper. Much as I don't want to, I'm going to have to apologize."

"Boss, if Cooper is out there, I can call off our search and get the boys to concentrate on the Russians. I got a feeling they're ready to pull something. I don't want any more problems here."

"You do that, Tony."

"Thanks for the promotion, boss. I won't let you down."

"You earned it. Just keep me in the picture."

Cameron called Torrance. He told him what he had just learned, and Torrance had to cut off a burst of laughter. He coughed loudly to cover his indiscretion.

"Sorry, Lou, it came as a shock to know Lonny did something right."

"How do you think I feel? Okay, Walt, we need to stop this guy before he makes his play. He didn't come all the way down here just to beef up his tan. This changes things. You and Lonny step up the search. I want this asshole on the ground in front of me. I want him alive but hurting. You understand me, Walt?"

"You got it, Lou," Torrance said. "What about the stuff you got out at the plant?"

"I been thinking about that. I'll call Calvera and tell him to pick it up. The sooner it's off my hands the better. I'll set up the loading and we can move out in the morning. Meet Calvera's plane at the pickup point. If there isn't anything on the shelf, this Cooper guy can't blow it up."

14

Erin Kowalski overheard Torrance's phone conversation by pure accident. The young deputy had been about to knock and enter Torrance's office, a request for shift approval in her hand, when the sheriff's raised voice caught her attention. It was the tone of Torrance's voice, part-defiant, part-deferential, that made her stop and concentrate on the discussion.

"...only one thing we can do, Lou. Get the mother out of town. On his own. We can handle it any way you want. Deal with him and dig a hole where no one can find him. Like you say, this is not a good time to have some loose cannon wandering around. If Cooper's the guy who did the number on your Chicago and Newark places, it stands to reason he's on a roll. Cameron Oil will be next. Let me and Lonny handle it from this end. Hell, it won't be the first time we made someone vanish. There's plenty of empty space to put him where he'll never be found."

Torrance stopped talking as the party on the other end of the line spoke. Although Kowalski couldn't make out the words, she could tell the speaker was raising his voice, asserting his position. He talked for some while before he allowed Torrance to continue.

"Okay, Lou, if that's what you want. We take him alive and deliver him to you at the ranch. Yeah, that's clear. So what do we do about this Russian thing? Okay, we keep a watch for them. Handle them if they show up. Fine, Lou, you're the boss. Talk to you soon."

As Torrance put the cell phone down Erin backed away from the office, stepping quickly into the department's armory, which was next to Torrance's office. She busied herself with her service revolver, quickly opening the cylinder and ejecting the loads onto the worktop.

She heard the solid sound of Torrance's boots as he left his office and walked past the armory door, pausing when he saw her.

"Isn't it time you were on patrol, Kowalski?"

She half turned, nodding. "In a couple of minutes, Sheriff. Just making sure my piece is clean. Dust seems to get everywhere."

Torrance took a half-step toward the door, his face set as he watched her wiping her revolver with a cloth. "You hear anyone out in the corridor?"

"No, sir. Is there a problem?" Her heart was thumping so loud she could have imagined Torrance might be able to hear it.

The sheriff stayed where he was for a few seconds, then grunted to himself and walked on. If Kowalski had been facing him fully, the man would have been able to see the sheen of sweat across her forehead. Close, she decided. Too damn close.

She reloaded the Magnum revolver and slipped it back in the holster, snapping the clip in place. She left the armory and walked back into the squad room, where a couple of the other deputies were busy at their desks. Eddie Phillips was at his control position. She patted him on the shoulder as she went by.

"I'll be on air in a minute," she said.

"On patrol?" he asked, knowing exactly what she was doing. The duty roster was on his notice board over his desk.

"Keeping McQueen County safe," she said, keeping her voice steady. She wanted to be out of the office, in her SUV cruiser where she could think straight.

She passed Lonny Magruder's desk and saw him glance up, his beefy face wearing the sly smirk he reserved only for her.

"You going to be okay out there, girl?" he asked, wetting his lips with the tip of his tongue. "I mean all on your lonesome with no one to hold your hand? We could partner up."

Kowalski stopped and placed both her palms flat against his desktop.

"Given the choice of putting myself at risk against having your pasty butt next to me, Deputy Magruder, guess which option I'd choose?"

Magruder's face darkened as he glared at her. It didn't help his mood when he heard a faint chuckle coming from one of his coworkers.

"Have a nice day, Lonny," Kowalski whispered and walked out.

Outside she unlocked the SUV, threw her hat on the passenger seat and climbed in. She fired up the big engine, swung the vehicle around and hung a right. She clicked on the com set and signed on with Eddie Phillips.

"Nicely handled," Phillips said. "Jeez, his face is still red. Erin, you keep your eyes open when he's around. You know how he is."

"Thanks for the advice, Eddie, and I *do* know how he is."

Kowalski cruised the street, heading out of town and onto the highway that led south. Clear of town she was able to sit back, with the smooth ribbon of the road stretching ahead. She was alone, with only the muted chatter of the radio to break the silence. It allowed her to concentrate her thoughts.

At this moment Kowalski needed the isolation as she tried to make sense of the conversation she had overheard.

It was obvious Torrance had been talking to Lou Cameron. It was a fact that McQueen's sheriff was a *good* friend of the Camerons. The brothers were well-known figures in town, often seen at the Cameron Oil office. The younger one, Nathan, made no secret of the fact that he had, as they said, taken a shine to the attractive young deputy. And while Kowalski made no overtly familiar response to his attention, she did nothing to offend him. He was a pleasant enough young man, unlike his brother. Kowalski found the elder Cameron distant, obsessed with his business and a man who had a habit of treating people with a cold attitude. He would be polite, but there was always that obvious disdain she found unsettling. He went around with a slightly mocking expression in his eyes.

Look at me. I'm better than you simple peasants.

Apart from the relationship Torrance had with Lou Cameron, Kowalski had long harbored a suspicion the sheriff's connection was more than simple friendship. Her father still reminded her, whenever conversation centered on Torrance, that he had always mistrusted the man. He had known the sheriff years back, when the man had first put on a uniform. That had been when Sam Kowalski had been in charge of the department. Torrance had made his way up through the ranks. He could have been an exceptional officer, but there was a darker side to him that occasionally came through. He had a heavy hand with prisoners and though he never crossed the line, there were occasions when Torrance came close. Sam Kowalski simply did not trust the man. When Sam was injured during a shooting that left him with a crippled hip, Torrance was elected to the top position. At the time he was the senior man in the department and he had *friends*.

Lou Cameron was at the head of the list. In the local business community Cameron had a lot of clout. His oil company provided jobs in the area, and he brought business to McQueen.

Sam Kowalski, by that time retired to Las Cruces, had not been pleased, and when his daughter had been taken on as a deputy, he warned her to stay on watch as far as Torrance was concerned.

"That son of a bitch is not to be trusted, and neither is Lonny Magruder," he had said. "That pair's like Siamese twins. Just keep your distance, honey. Watch and listen, 'cause one day they are going to let something slip."

Erin Kowalski had a feeling that day had come.

She ran back over the conversation she had been privy to.

No matter how she juggled the words they always came out the same.

Torrance had been suggesting he and Magruber kill some-one and bury him in the desert out beyond McQueen—Cooper, the man Magruder had clashed with after he had pulled him over. It had gone all around the department after Torrance had bawled him out over the incident. Now that same guy appears to have been targeted for assassination.

Kowalski tried to convince herself she had mistaken the con-versation, but she failed because Torrance's words could not be interpreted any other way. His inappropriate discussion over the phone simply advertised his lack of tact. That failing was typical of the man. Walt Torrance believed himself to be total master of his own fate. So much so that he failed to censor him-self and walked around with the air of someone untouchable.

Not this time, Sheriff Torrance, she thought.

Cooper.

The newcomer to McQueen seemed to be attracting a great deal of hostile attention.

Why?

Torrance and Cameron had been discussing the man and arranging for him to be either snatched off the street—or even killed if that turned out to be the only solution.

Whoever Cooper was there had to be a backstory, a logical explanation for Torrance's determination to get his hands on the man.

Kowalski had to unearth that explanation. To do it she had to confront the man and ask the question. Something drove her to seek the answer. If she got that answer she might not like it, but her dogged need to know would not allow her to just ignore the matter.

She picked up the vehicle's handset and keyed the button.

"Erin? You okay?" Phillips asked.

"Are you on your own?"

"Weird question, but yes. Is it important?"

"Could be. Did Lonny log, Cooper, that guy he pulled over?" Kowalski asked.

"He called it in, sure."

"You got the details?"

"Hold a minute." Kowalski could hear him tapping on his keyboard. "I got the log."

"Send it to my computer, Eddie, and don't ask why. I'll tell you later. And keep this between us."

Phillips agreed and Kowalski signed off from the conversation.

When the details appeared on her screen, she ran through them. Magruder, as unpleasant as he was, was a stickler for keeping his logs up to date. He had detailed everything that had occurred at the roadside, putting down his report in full. He had activated the video camera mounted inside the patrol vehicle and had pasted a photograph from the footage into his log. It gave Kowalski a recognizable image of the man named Matt Cooper. The tall, dark-haired man had looked calm, not even a little stressed at being pulled over. Kowalski smiled when she saw that. It would have irritated Magruder because the guy had not reacted. The log gave the make and number of the SUV Cooper was driving. She ran a check on the plate number and the information came through. The SUV had been hired from a rental agency in Las Cruces.

"So far so good, my girl," Kowalski said out loud.

She had increased her knowledge a little. What did it all add up to? She wasn't quite sure yet. So she needed to keep pushing.

Her radio squawked. It was Eddie Phillips.

"Torrance and Magruder just left the department," he said. "After you left they put their heads together for a while, then they took off without a word. They were acting weird, Erin. Thought I'd give you the heads-up."

"Thanks, Eddie."

"Erin, what the hell is going on out there?" Phillips asked.

"Beats the hell out of me, but I'm going to find out."

"You watch yourself. Especially around Lonny. I don't trust him."

"Message loud and clear, Eddie," Kowalski stated.

"You keep in touch."

15

Bolan sat in his SUV, having decided to wait until dark before he moved forward with his plan of action. The turnoff leading to Cameron Oil was a couple of miles along the blacktop. He had parked alongside the deserted diner and gas station he had passed on his previous trip along the road. The old gas station and diner looked to have been abandoned a long time ago—the weather-beaten paintwork, faded signs and the general air of decay told the story. Grass had long ago established itself in the cracked concrete. The regular winds that blew in the area had carried the grains of dust that had scoured the property.

Bolan had pulled in beside the diner, with its sagging sign and broken windows, reversing the SUV so he was facing the road. There were a couple of hours to fill before darkness would help cover his approach to the processing plant. A simple recon would confirm his suspicions one way or the other.

The road was quiet. Only a couple of vehicles drove by while Bolan sat out his vigil.

The third vehicle he saw caused Bolan to let go a sigh of exasperation. It was an SUV bearing the McQueen County Sheriff's Department logo and had the requisite light bar mounted on the roof.

So you took a chance and it just blew back in your face, Bolan thought.

He was considering his options as the vehicle slowed,

turned off the road and parked in front of the gas pumps. The uniformed driver of the cruiser climbed out and stood for a moment, staring across at Bolan's SUV.

At least it wasn't Deputy Magruder. Bolan wasn't seeing the bulk of the man. He was looking at a lithe young woman who did everything good to the uniform—everything that Magruder did not. She started to walk in his direction. She moved well, almost casually, but there was no denying the power she carried under her uniform. Bolan climbed out of his vehicle and stepped around to the front, both hands held well away from his body as the woman kept coming. As she got closer, he realized that she was strikingly attractive. Her thick, raven-black hair was cut reasonably short, and her intense gray-green eyes demanded attention. The badge she wore on her tan, short-sleeved uniform shirt was pinned above the name tag that told Bolan she was Deputy Kowalski.

"Deputy," Bolan said pleasantly. He maintained his relaxed stance, offering no aggression, no resistance.

Kowalski returned the favor. Although her right hand was low and near the butt of her holstered service revolver, her fingers were curled into a partial fist. It was not the position of someone anticipating the need to draw her weapon.

As she drew near, Bolan picked up on detail. Her skin was smooth, unmarked, her mouth generous, with full lips. Her brows were dark above the unflinching and clear eyes.

"Watching the scenery, Mr. Cooper?"

Bolan didn't react. He saw the flicker of amusement on her lips at his coolness.

"Or waiting until it gets dark?"

Smart, too, he decided.

"Photographers love sunsets. They make for good shots."

"They also let people move around without being seen."

"Not much around here to be seen in the dark, Deputy Kowalski."

"That depends what you're looking for."

"Is every officer on the local force interested in what I do?"

That quick smile again. "Some more than others," she said. "And for different reasons."

"Deputy Magruder?" Bolan nodded. "We met earlier. He gets upset easily."

"Well, now you have his best buddy, Sheriff Torrance, on your case."

"As far as I'm aware, I haven't broken any county bylaws. Unless you can tell me different."

"Mr. Cooper, I don't have a clue what's behind all this. I just know you're in possible danger."

"Can you explain that remark?"

"I overheard Torrance on the phone arranging your kidnapping or possible murder with—"

Bolan had the feeling he knew the name the young woman was going to say. "Lou Cameron?"

It was Kowalski's turn to be caught off guard. She was not as practical at concealing her surprise as Bolan, and it showed on her face.

"How did you…"

The intrusive squeal of tires interrupted her. A second cruiser swept onto view, jerking to a dusty stop only feet away. The driver's door swung open and the bulky figure of Deputy Magruder stepped out, the black muzzle of a pump-action shotgun pointing at Bolan.

"You move one fucking inch, Cooper, and I'll blow you into dog meat."

16

"What the hell is going on, Lonny?" Kowalski asked. She rounded on the deputy. "I want to know."

"Yeah? Well, I don't need to tell you nothing, sweetheart. I knew one day that poking your nose in where it wasn't wanted would get you trouble. Just get that tight little butt of yours turned around and shut your mouth."

It dawned on Kowalski that her curiosity was proving to have been validated. Just seeing Magruder's sweating face and twitchy mouth said it all.

"Move it," the deputy snapped, his tone hardening.

Kowalski glared at Bolan. "You figure this is right?"

"Hate to say this, but right doesn't matter. He does have the shotgun."

"That's right, and I know how to use it," Magruder snapped. "Move, Kowalski."

"Lonny, what will the sheriff say about this?" Kowalski asked innocently. "He isn't going to be happy."

The man just grinned at her. "He'll most likely give me a bonus. Just stop jerking around and let's get moving."

"My God," Kowalski said. "I did hear correct. You bastards do work for Cameron."

The look on Magruder's face told her she was right. The revelation momentarily put him off guard, the shotgun sagging in his hands. Kowalski reached for her holstered pistol, but Magruder was too quick. He swung the shotgun, the barrel rapping her knuckles, and she let go of the pistol as it slid free of the holster. Kowalski gasped, clutching her bruised knuckles, but she lashed out with one booted foot and caught Magruder a hard blow to the left knee.

"Son of a bitch," he said and swung his shotgun at her.

She ducked under the swing, giving Bolan a chance to lunge forward. He saw the shotgun reverse and head in his direction. The soldier arched his body away from the weapon and it brushed his side. He threw up his left arm to block Magruder's follow-up swing, feeling the solid impact of the barrel as it struck.

"Lonny, no," Kowalski yelled, moving to intercept the deputy's assault.

"The hell you say," Magruder said, backhanding her with a beefy fist. "Stay out of my way, girlie, or else I'm gonna teach you some manners, too."

As the deputy went to her knees, Magruder lashed out with his shotgun again, this time catching Bolan across the back of his shoulders. The blow was delivered with less than full strength. It stung, but didn't put Bolan down. Out the corner of his eye Bolan saw the weapon rise again, and he ducked under Magruder's arm and slammed in a hard fist that landed just above the deputy's belt buckle. There was a softness there that told Bolan the man got little exercise. He drove in with his left, sinking it deep into Magruder's unprotected gut.

The deputy let out a gush of air, took a short step back as he tried to regain control. Bolan was not in a waiting mood. He straightened and launched a big fist that crunched against the man's slack jaw. The blow rocked Magruder's head. He tasted blood in his mouth from a loosened tooth. Knowing that if the officer regained his wits he might use the shotgun, Bolan struck again, hard, and punched in over the ribs, then slammed his fist against Magruder's jaw a second time. This time he went down, spitting blood and flopping on his face, letting go of the shotgun. Bolan snatched it up. Then he reached down and took Magruder's pistol from his holster and tossed it away from the deputy.

Hé turned to Officer Kowalski. She was already pushing upright, watching Bolan. She had seen him remove Magruder's gun and throw it out of reach. It posed a problem for her. A genuine fugitive would have taken the gun and made his escape. Instead he was standing over her, extending a helping hand to haul her upright, the shotgun held in a nonthreatening position. She moved her right hand as if she was going to take out her own weapon, then remembered it was on the ground. But something inside told her she had nothing to fear from this man.

"Some partner you have there," Bolan said.

Kowalski touched her fingertips to the spot on her cheek where Magruder had hit her. "That guy is so far back he should be dragging his knuckles on the ground," she said. "Ouch, that's going to hurt."

"It is," Bolan said. "Are you going to be okay?"

"I'll be fine." She grinned. "The Kowalskis are a tough breed."

"Tough and stubborn as a fuckin' burro. Just like your bastard of a father."

Kowalski knew the voice. She turned and faced Sheriff Torrance. He had stepped into view from the corner of the building. He had a big, black Franchi SPAS shotgun aimed directly at her head. Behind him the tail end of his cruiser stuck out from the side of the building. He had driven up quietly while Bolan and Kowalski were dealing with Magruder, giving himself the advantage.

"Torrance."

"Tell your man there to lay down that shotgun. I can get a shot in before he can, and this here piece will take your head clear off your shoulders."

Bolan knew the cop was right. No matter how fast he might be, Torrance was in a better position. And the soldier knew, even if he had the chance, there was no way he would fire on a law officer, even if he was crooked. Corrupt or not, Torrance's position would keep him safe from Bolan's weapons. He lowered the shotgun to the ground. Magruder, bloodied and groggy, was climbing to his feet and scooping up the weapon.

"Let me take him, Walt," he said. "I want to finish him."

Torrance moved closer, gesturing with his shotgun for Bolan and Kowalski to step back against the side of her cruiser.

"No. Cameron wants this son of a bitch alive." The ragged laugh coming from the sheriff sounded as if he was really enjoying himself. "Cooper, he is going to be a happy man when I drop you in his lap."

"I can't believe you'd do this," Kowalski said and felt foolish the moment she spoke.

"Think I give a damn what you believe?" Torrance said. "You figure you're so smart. It's been going on right under your nose all the time, and you didn't see it. How dumb does that make you, Deputy?"

Kowalski's cheeks flushed with anger. Bolan admired the way she refused to back down from his smug expression.

"Sheriff, I feel sick just looking at you wearing that badge. You and Magruder are scum. If I had my gun right—"

"Well, you don't, missy. Lonny took it away from you."

Magruder gave a snort of laughter. He used his shirtsleeve to scrub at the mess of blood dribbling down his chin. "That's right, Deputy." He leaned in close, his eyes bright with some secret thought. "But if you want I got something in my pants you could hold."

If revulsion had been a lethal emotion, Magruder would have been dead in the dirt at that moment, Bolan realized.

The words were barely out of his mouth when Kowalski looked him square in the face. "The way I heard it, Lonny, what you do have in there isn't worth the effort of handling."

The man's face suffused with color. He let out a screech of anger, lunging at Kowalski, all caution evaporating in that moment. As he moved, he slid his nightstick free and slashed it around, clipping her across one cheek. She twisted aside and in that hectic moment Bolan saw, and took, the window of opportunity she had opened for him.

He powered away from the front of his SUV, slamming into Magruder and catapulting him directly into Torrance's path. The two collided, Magruder's nightstick flailing and cracking across the bridge of the sheriff's nose. Torrance bellowed in pain, tears filling his eyes and blood squirting from his nose. Bolan followed up behind Magruder. He slammed his open palm against the back of the deputy's skull, ramming his head forward to connect with Torrance's face. The entangled pair stumbled, attempting to separate themselves from each other. Bolan drove a booted foot into the back of Magruder's left leg, collapsing it and the deputy yelled, sagging as his leg went from under him. Torrance shook his head, spraying blood in a wide arc. He lifted the SPAS, tracking in on Bolan's moving figure.

The Executioner swept his right palm forward and knocked the shotgun barrel to the side in the instant before Torrance pulled the trigger. The SPAS exploded with sound, the deadly shot cleaving thin air. Bolan wrapped his hands around the weapon, twisted and broke the sheriff's grip on the shotgun. He let it fall to the ground, straight-armed Torrance with his left hand and lashed out with a brutal backhand that rolled the sheriff around. Bolan snatched the pistol from Torrance's holster and bounced it off the man's skull, driving Torrance to his knees.

Behind Bolan a pained grunt erupted from Magruder's lips as Kowalski stepped in close and booted him across the side of his head. She bent and picked up her pistol and followed in Bolan's shadow. He grabbed the fallen SPAS, turned and blew out the tires on Magruder's cruiser, then did the same to Torrance's.

"Let's go," Bolan said. He yanked open the door of his rental, dropped the shotgun and Torrance's handgun on the cab floor and slid behind the wheel. Kowalski ran around and climbed into the passenger seat as the Executioner fired up the engine. Tires screeched as he drove the SUV away from the scene, bouncing over the curb before he hit the highway. He floored the gas pedal, feeling the powerful engine surge. The big SUV sped along the empty road, Bolan ignoring warning signs and speed restrictions.

"I should be writing you a whole stack of tickets," Kowalski said. "We try to encourage safe driving in McQueen."

Bolan glanced at her and saw she had a slight smile on her lips. "Deputy, you have a strange sense of humor."

"My dad's always telling me that. So where are we going, Cooper? My place, or yours?"

"For the time being we stay away from both," Bolan said.

Kowalski took a moment to look around, running her hands through her thick hair. "Dammit, Cooper, what the hell is going on? Since you showed up in McQueen County, it's turned crazy. First Lonny, then Torrance gunning for you—like you were some psycho on the run from solitary." She glared at Bolan. "You're not on the run, are you? Just what is your story?"

"Deputy—Erin—I can't prove anything yet. All I can tell you is what I know. Lou Cameron and his brother Nathan head an organized crime syndicate dealing in illegal weapons. They supply whatever their clients want. Lately they've started pushing hijacked military ordnance to customers in Chicago and Newark. I came into this after Miami cops were slaughtered on the city streets by warring gangs. Those gang members were armed with military-grade automatic weapons. The cops were outgunned and didn't stand a chance. Those weapons were brokered by Cameron's organization."

"It was you," Kowalski said. "News media had it all over the networks. Hits in Chicago and Newark—the police found dead street hoods at both places and weapons that had been destroyed. They said it must have been gangs taking each other down, but no one could figure out why the weapons were destroyed. It didn't make sense, but it does now. I'm right, Cooper. That's why you came down here to McQueen County. To take Cameron out of the game. It's why Torrance has been after you. I only just found out earlier today that Torrance and Magruder are working for Cameron. Torrance took a phone call from Cameron to have you snatched, or killed. Tell me I'm wrong, Cooper."

"That's why I'm here, Erin. Cameron and his organization are selling weapons to any criminal who can come up with the money. He doesn't give a damn what happens once he makes his deals. The law is having a hard time getting the goods on him because he's protected on all sides. He can afford the best legal defense to run rings around the law-enforcement agencies. Plus he's buying interference in the form of crooked cops like Torrance and Magruder."

"You must think I'm so stupid," Kowalski said bitterly. "I was right there, working with them and didn't see a damn thing."

"Don't be so hard on yourself. Torrance will have everything tied up because he's the lead cop in the department. He can cover for Cameron, make problems disappear. He has the clout to control what information comes and goes."

"Then he's been pulling the strings of every cop in McQueen. Dammit, Cooper, he made fools of us all."

"Work on the assumption you can't trust anyone. Go by your own instincts. In a situation like this it's the only way to survive."

"Is that how you work, Cooper? You don't trust anyone? *Anyone?*"

"It's a selective option, Erin," Bolan said, smiling at her question.

The deputy settled back in her seat, staring out through the windshield, lost in thought. Bolan concentrated on his driving and left Kowalski to whatever was demanding her attention. He felt her conclusion might be running along the lines he was looking at himself.

"It has to be the plant," she said without preamble, breaking her silence. "Cameron Oil."

"I'm listening," Bolan said. She had reached the same conclusion as he had.

"Twenty miles out of town—more or less in desert country. Cameron has a fleet of tankers that collect and deliver. They can move in any direction. Even across the border into Mexico. Cooper, it's an ideal setup for transporting illegal cargo. There's most likely a storage area for the ordnance within the plant." Kowalski glanced at Bolan, willing him to respond. "Well? Doesn't it make sense?"

"Could be."

"Wow, how are you keeping your enthusiasm under such control?" The sarcasm was strong in her voice.

"I'm not trying to dismiss it, Erin. I think you've hit on something. Same as me."

"So what are we going to do about it? And before you even consider it, I'm not walking away. This is you and me. All the way. Torrance made a mistake when he figured me for just a girl with a gun. I don't enjoy feeling that I've been treated like an idiot."

"I can see that," Bolan said. "Just remember these people play for keeps. The fact you're a woman won't buy you any favors."

"Okay, since we've established that, what next?"

"I think that visit to check out Cameron Oil is still on the cards."

"Let me show you how we can sneak in around the blind side, then, Cooper."

17

There was a full moon, enabling Bolan to drive without lights. Kowalski proved she knew the territory well. She guided him with uncanny accuracy, bringing them to within a half mile of Cameron Oil, by way of trails that barely seemed to exist. They had been driving for almost three hours when she brought him to a stop. Bolan killed the engine. The silence out here in the rugged, empty desert was absolute.

"You know your territory."

"Being born here and having a father who's a cop helps."

"Yeah."

"Now we walk," she said.

The Executioner went around to the rear of the SUV and raised the door. He slid his equipment bag to the edge of the space and opened it. Even in the pale light from the full moon Kowalski could see the weapons collection. While Bolan set himself up she examined his ordnance with a professional eye.

"Cooper, you could start a war with all this."

"This *is* a war," he said. "And it has to be fought."

The conviction in his voice made her realize just how serious he was. He was no vigilante with a death wish. He was a man dedicated to his mission, and she saw he would fight it with every fiber of his being. She could have plagued him with questions about who he really was. Why he was involved. An endless barrage of queries. She didn't. Surprisingly, Kowalski held back. For one thing this was not the time to interrogate him. What they were doing was risky enough. The last thing she wanted to do was to throw him off balance with, what he would consider, irritating probing. On reflection, she decided it would take more than female curiosity to take his mind off his upcoming business. So she stayed silent.

From the corner of her eye she saw him peel off his outer clothing to reveal the one-piece blacksuit. He pulled on sturdy boots, then a combat harness. There was a shoulder rig that held a pistol she didn't recognize, then a waist belt with a holster for a big Desert Eagle on one side and a sheathed knife on the other. She saw the competent way he checked each handgun, adding extra magazines to the pouches on the harness. A 9 mm Uzi was slung across his back. He worked quietly, efficiently, with the ease of a seasoned warrior, and she suspected that somewhere in his past he had been a combat soldier. The training they received stayed with them, an awareness that survival depended on being ready at all times. Her dad had been a Marine, and the values he had absorbed flowed over into civilian life, so watching Bolan, Kowalski understood in part what drove him.

Commitment.

Loyalty.

The ingrained dedication to a cause.

Satisfied with his gear, Bolan reached into his war bag and eased out an M-4 A-1 rifle. He located an SAI M80 sound suppressor and screwed it into place before handing the rifle to Kowalski. He didn't have to ask if she was familiar with the weapon as she checked it, tapping the full magazine he gave her on the solid edge of the vehicle pillar before snapping it in place. Loosening the 5.56 mm cartridges to prevent possible seizure was an old military trick. Bolan suspected her father had taught her that. With the M-4 cocked and locked, the deputy waited for his orders.

"We go in quiet," Bolan said. "When I say to, you take position and cover my back. You don't come any closer. I need to reach the perimeter fence so I can make my recon."

"Will you go inside?"

"That depends on what I get from a close check. If Torrance has told Cameron about our encounter, there could be increased activity. If there is, it might work in our favor and show us more than we expected." Bolan studied her face. "If you think this is more than you can handle, Erin, say so now and you can stay here by the vehicle."

"If we'd known each other for longer, that question wouldn't even come up. I won't quit on you, Cooper."

"If it does get hot and you need to defend yourself, I have only one rule. Hit the other guy before he takes his shot. No remorse. No hesitation. Remember he's going to be thinking the same. Worry later. Combat is like living. You get one run at it. Screw it up there's no going back for a redo. Understand?"

Kowalski nodded. "Cooper, you're a bundle of laughs."

Bolan touched her shoulder, then led the way out.

The lights of the plant stood out in the desert gloom. Powerful lamps threw shafts of illumination beyond the perimeter fences, so it was no hardship for Bolan and Kowalski when it came to getting a fix on their target. As promised, the deputy had brought them in by the back door, with the western section of the high fence directly ahead.

They had, as well as the near-dark conditions, plenty of natural cover from the local vegetation—patches of creosote bush, mesquite, stands of cactus and yucca. The soft ground allowed them easy passage as they neared the perimeter fence.

At four hundred yards Bolan stopped, crouching low to the ground. He could see movement beyond the steel fence. There were men and vehicles, with plenty of activity taking place. Kowalski took up her position slightly behind Bolan. She could see the same scene and refrained from speaking while she observed. Bolan had taken his powerful monocular from a pocket, using it to get a closer look at what was happening. The strong lights inside the fence gave him a clear picture, and he found he was able to see far more than he might have expected.

The familiar configuration of boxes and crates were being lifted from what seemed to be a concrete bunker set low to the ground. The bunker was set close to the western section of the plant, away from the main production area where a maze of pipe and storage tanks was situated. Cameron had his illegal operation set inside the plant, as Bolan and Kowalski had figured. And right before their eyes he was moving what appeared to be a considerable amount of cargo.

Was it because Cameron had been warned of Bolan's presence? Had he taken note and decided to shift his cache of weapons to another location? It was entirely possible this was nothing more than a normal run for Cameron. Shifting goods to be delivered to a client? Whatever was really going on, Bolan had struck gold.

"They're loading up for a run," he said to Kowalski. "You stay here and cover my back. I want to get closer to make a definite ID."

"Be careful," the deputy said.

She bellied down, the M-4 A-1 cradled in her arms as she watched Bolan crawl away into the shadows. She followed his progress as he edged in toward the fence.

THE UNEVEN TERRAIN made it easier for Bolan to work his way to within inches of the perimeter fence. He was able to position himself at a point where the vehicle loading was within fifteen feet. He scanned the scene.

The dozen-strong crew was fully armed. Those doing the loading wore handguns while the rest carried SMGs. Bolan recognized Cameron and his brother, Nathan, supervising the loading of the cargo into a long wheelbase heavy-duty panel truck. The vehicle was fitted with wide tires for travel over the desert terrain. Parked nearby were two high-end 4x4s. Escort vehicles.

Bolan was within earshot of Cameron and his brother and picked up their conversation.

"…where did Cooper go?"

"Good question," Cameron said. "If he figures he's been exposed, probably gone to ground. Suits me until we get this cargo on its way to Calvera. Then we can concentrate on hunting the mother down."

"You had any more news from back east?"

"Nothing."

"Fuck, Lou, we had things running great until that bastard Cooper showed up and started blowing everything to hell. Then Poliokof starts jumping around and cutting our people down."

"That's been expected for a time," Cameron said. "The Russians have been waiting for their chance. Cooper jump-started things and Poliokof saw his opportunity."

One of the armed men walked over to Cameron.

"That's everything loaded, boss."

Cameron nodded. "Tell the boys to rest up. Move out at first light. Rendezvous with Calvera's crew at the airstrip at ten. His plane will be there by then. Close the deal and get back here."

"Why Lender air base?" Nathan asked.

"Because it's got a good stretch of runway for that transport Calvera runs. It's isolated, and it's been closed since the Air Force cut back. Quit worrying, brother, and let's get back home."

Cameron instructed his crew to close up and move out. As they drifted away, Bolan reversed his approach and made his way back to where Kowalski waited patiently.

"Abandoned Air Force base called Lender. You know it?"

"South," she said. "About four hours from here."

"That's where Cameron's delivering to someone called Calvera. Rendezvous is for ten tomorrow morning."

"I know the way they'll need to go. It's the only half-decent track in the area." She regarded him for a moment. "You think they'll make it?"

"Not a chance," Bolan said.

And he meant it.

18

Bolan ran a final check of his weapons. It was a purely reflex action coming from the warrior mentality. No fighting man could be accused of taking that matter lightly. Weapon malfunction in the heat of battle could end in disaster. So the Executioner, who had survived years of intense confrontation and high odds of defeat, understood the need to ensure his ordnance was in pristine condition. He laid his M72 LAW single-shot missiles beside him, each one close at hand for the moment when he might need them.

Then he waited, checking his watch to see how much time he had. If he had gauged it correctly, the delivery convoy should be well on its way. He figured, give or take a few minutes, he should be sighting the vehicles anytime.

Bolan could feel the risen sun on his back. He moved the LAWs into the shadow cast by the rocks he was concealed behind. Despite the baseball cap, the heat made his scalp itch. A bead of sweat eased from behind one ear and trickled annoyingly down his neck.

Kowalski was concealed in a spread of dusty rocks a hundred feet behind. She had accepted her role to watch his back with good grace.

Bolan saw the lead vehicle as it nosed into view from a dip in the dusty track. Behind it was the laden panel truck, albeit with a longer wheelbase allowing extra load space. Despite its

heavy-duty springs, the rear of the truck lay low due to the
cargo it was carrying. Bolan allowed himself a thin smile as he
anticipated his next move, which would relieve the truck of its
heavy load.

His earlier recon of the immediate area had given him the
range for his strike. There were less than twenty-five yards
between Bolan's hiding place and the ill-defined road. This
wouldn't be the first time he had used the M72, and he knew
the weapon's capabilities. With his targets in sight, the soldier
reached for the first missile and snapped out the extension tube
that cocked the launcher as it clicked into place. With the LAW
resting across his right shoulder, Bolan tracked the lead vehicle,
hands and fingers in place. He fired, feeling the tremor as the
missile's charge built, then propelled it from the tube with a
solid whoosh of sound.

The thin vapor trail marked the rocket as it sped across the
open space, the stabilizing fins having snapped into place as it
left the tube. The missile tip struck midway along the vehicle.
The detonation shattered the silence. Bolan saw the 4x4 vanish
in a deadly burst of flame, the impact tearing it apart. The
vehicle was lifted off the ground under the force of the explosion, and debris scattered as the blazing hulk dropped back to
earth.

Bolan already had his second launcher in place, this time
targeting the main vehicle as it jerked to a stop. He hit the trigger, sending his follow-up missile on its fiery journey. Like an
instant replay, the missile struck and blew the panel truck into
a pulsing fireball. The difference was the secondary explosion
as munitions detonated, adding a crackling, intense burst that
consumed the bulk of the vehicle. As the truck came apart,
Bolan saw a helpless figure ejected from the maelstrom. It
spun, engulfed in flame, and hit the ground, jerking for agoniz-
ing seconds before it became still. A rain of debris began to fall
to earth, shadowed by the rising pall of smoke from the burning
wreck. Occasional crackles from ammunition still sounded.

Bolan pulled back from his position as he spotted the third
vehicle speed into view. He had been expecting backup. He

reached for his remaining LAW, loaded it and turned it in the direction of the SUV as it swerved around the burning wrecks. Bolan fired head-on, but the driver spun the wheel and the powerful vehicle made a harsh turn. The missile missed by inches, hitting the ground well behind the target, throwing a thick geyser of earth into the air as the 4x4 came to a slithering stop. Doors opened, disgorging a five-man, armed crew that scattered, weapons up and chattering as they targeted Bolan's position. He ducked behind cover as slugs pounded his protecting rocks, spitting shards of stone over him as he pulled back.

The Executioner stayed low as he moved, aware that the crew had the numbers to outflank him if he remained static. He had taken the M-4 A-1 this time, giving Kowalski the Uzi. He unlimbered the rifle, moved the selector switch to three-round bursts, and used the protecting curve of the rocks to maintain his cover. That wouldn't last for long. The upthrusting wall of rocks petered out after so many yards, and once that was gone he would become exposed before he could reach his concealed SUV.

Bad odds, but the notion of possible defeat never once entered Bolan's thoughts. He didn't work that way. He had to remain positive, pushing ahead on the premise that life meant too much to even consider giving in. His battle against evil was never ending—so life *had* to continue.

He caught movement to his right as one of the crew made a brazen attempt to get the drop on the quarry. The guy scrambled up across the rocks, his intention to get a clear shot at the Executioner. Bolan swiveled at the hips, his M-4 A-1 angling up and delivering twin three-round bursts that punched in at gut level. The target lurched, a short gasp bursting from his lips as his flesh was punctured and the 5.56 mm slugs ripped at his internal organs. He stumbled back into empty air and crashed to the ground out of Bolan's sight.

The soldier kept moving. He had little choice. With the crew having spread out, there was no easy way to deal with them. He heard a shout from behind as one hardman came around the far

end of the rocks, calling to his partners, and at the same time
warning Bolan of his presence.

Thanks for that, Bolan thought, and turned, dropping to one
knee. His fingers moved the selector to semiauto even as he
brought the combat rifle to his shoulder and sighted in on the
running man. He held the moving target for a couple of seconds
even as the guy swung his own SMG into position. His finger
eased back on the M-4 A-1's trigger. The rifle fired and the
unwary crewman went down with a 5.56 mm slug in his heart.

Bolan was upright and turned around as the brass shell hit
the ground. With the selector switch back on three-round burst,
he moved on.

Two down.

Three to go.

The end of the rock barrier was ahead, and open, undulating
ground lay beyond.

A flicker of movement came into his line of vision. A pair of
gunners bolted around the final grouping of rocks.

The lead guy opened fire the instant he saw Bolan. His shots
were close, kicking up dirt feet away. The soldier returned fire.
A miss, but the effect was to scatter the pair as they realized
the vulnerable position *they* were in, too.

Bolan saw a deep depression just ahead. He loosed another burst, then dropped, slamming down and rolling into the
hollow, dust billowing up around him. As he went prone, M-4
thrust forward, he peered over the lip of the depression and saw
the two men, ten feet apart, coming at him in a wild rush. They
were firing on the run, peppering the earth with slugs, kicking
up dust.

The M-4 crackled and sent alternate bursts at the pair. Bolan
saw one jerk sideways, his midsection bloody. As he went to his
knees, the soldier hit him with a second trio, this time higher,
and the guy's throat suddenly turned into a bloody mess.

A burn of pain creased Bolan's left side. He swung the rifle
around and hit the second guy as he loomed large on the lip
of the depression. The gunner yelled as Bolan's burst clawed
into his torso, punching him off stride. His finger worked his

own weapon, and the Executioner felt the ground vibrate as slugs struck around him. Cameron's goon was on his knees, his face twisted in agony, his eyes staring at Bolan. He went to lift his SMG again, but his actions were lethargic. He jerked sideway as an Uzi stuttered a line of 9 mm slugs into him. He toppled backward and Bolan turned his head and saw Kowalski, only yards away, her face set and pale as she lowered the SMG.

There was sudden silence. Bolan became aware of his own breathing, the rise of pain from the wound in his side. He touched the area and his fingers came away stained with blood.

Damn.

He rolled onto his back against the slope of the depression, forcing his hands to remain steady as he ejected the M-4's magazine and replaced it with a fresh one.

He had not forgotten there was one more armed crewman.

"Get cover," he called to Kowalski. "One more out there."

She nodded and drew herself into a dusty hollow.

Easing to the lip of the depression, Bolan scanned the area and picked up the moving figure. The surviving gunner was heading in the direction of the backup vehicle. That was not what Bolan wanted. If the guy made it to the SUV, he was going to call in reinforcements.

Bolan pushed to his feet and took off after the guy, aware of his bleeding side but knowing he was going to have to isolate the pain until later.

Ahead of him the gunner turned to check behind and saw Bolan. He lifted his SMG and sent a burst of fire in Bolan's direction. The slugs marked a ragged line of hits in the dirt. The guy pulled himself to a stop, lined up for another burst. His finger hit the trigger. The 9 mm slugs cleared his target's left shoulder as Bolan fired his own return shots, a triburst impacting against the crewman's chest and knocking him back. The Executioner fired again, placing his slugs dead center and the gunner half turned as his legs went from beneath him. Dust feathered upward as he slammed facedown. The SMG flew from his slack grasp and cartwheeled across the ground.

"Clear," Bolan called.

Kowalski stood up and made her way to him.

Bolan clamped his hand to his side, pressing hard to try to stop the blood flow. He headed for the 4x4. The engine was still running. Bolan reached in and cut it. In the silence he leaned against the side of the big vehicle and propped his rifle against it, taking a moment.

"Let me see if they have a first-aid box on board," Kowalski said.

She checked the SUV and located what she was looking for under the passenger seat. She placed it on the vehicle hood and opened the box while Bolan peeled his blacksuit to his waist. She inspected the wound after pulling on a pair of latex gloves, her fingers gentle with the ragged, six-inch tear.

"From the scars, I'd say this kind of thing happens to you often," she stated.

"It comes with the territory."

"Cooper, you're not Superman. Well, I'm not sure who you are, but I don't see tights and a cape. So how long are you expecting to stay alive carrying on like this?"

As she spoke she was cleaning the torn flesh with gauze and an antiseptic salve that stung wildly.

"I figure I'm doing okay if I wake up every morning," Bolan said in a matter-of-fact tone.

In truth he understood what lay behind her question. His survival in the hell grounds was not a finite thing. Bolan counted himself lucky each time he walked away from the latest brush with death. He was driven by his need to make his life count for something. To face and defeat his enemies, whoever they were and wherever they showed up.

From the first pull of a trigger in his ongoing war, Bolan had expected to have a short life expectancy. Even after the many years he'd been fighting his war, he still expected a sudden end to it all. Not the thoughts of a defeatist, just the rationale of a mortal man willing himself to move on—to walk that extra mile. He knew he was pushing his luck to the limit.

The Executioner understood the need to maintain his will to fight on. His victories removed small numbers over the big picture, he understood that well enough, too. He still faced the next hurdle, and the next, because he had no other choice. If he quit, who would stand up to the evil that man heaped on his fellow man? Who would get payback for the Emily Crocketts of the world?

Kowalski covered the wound with gauze pads, then bound a bandage around his body, securing it tightly.

"Cooper, this isn't going to last too long," she said. "We need to get you to a hospital so you can have it treated and stitched."

"Nurse Kowalski, you are a lifesaver," Bolan said, pulling his blacksuit back into place.

The deputy closed the box. "We'll take this along," she said, "in case you need more attention."

"Thanks for the help."

"You do realize that Cameron is going to lose it when he finds out what you did?"

"Losing it isn't the best mood to be in to make decisions," Bolan said. "So I hope he loses it big-time."

19

"What do we do?"

Poliokof slammed his fist against the desk. "We take Cameron's business apart. Piece by piece. Man by man. I want Cameron and his organization to vanish. Everything he has becomes ours. We start to hit them now. Do it fast. Don't let them think about it."

They'd started with the Chicago and Newark bases. The Russians moved in swiftly and efficiently. First against Cameron's people. They were taken off the streets, from the outlets. Bundled into cars and panel trucks and driven away. There were no prior warnings. No ransom or negotiating demands. Over a period of twenty-four hours, the Chicago and Newark crews ceased to exist. Some were gunned down on the street, others turned up dead in alleys, or garbage Dumpsters at the rear of Cameron establishments. A number were never seen or heard from again.

THE POLICE IN BOTH Newark and Chicago were inundated with complaints from the public at the sudden escalation of indiscriminate violence, even though that violence was within the criminal fraternity. Behind closed doors the local cops might have been relieved that this was gang-related crime, with one group taking down another. But in public they had to decry the actions and state that they would be actively seeking the perpetrators.

In Newark Captain Ben Cahill understood the genesis of the incidents. The man he knew as Matt Cooper, the guy responsible for the partial destruction of the late Nicky Costanza's operation, had been instrumental in kicking off the current gang war. Stirring the pot had brought Poliokof's Russian Mob into play. Cooper as a catalyst was working fine. As long as the perps kept their in-fighting between themselves, Cahill wasn't about to lose any sleep.

IN CHICAGO Tony Lorenzo saw the matter from a different perspective. Sent by Cameron to oversee the situation in Chicago and Newark, the damage being done to the organization did his reputation little good. Cameron had trusted his lieutenant to get things under control. The sudden, unexpected surge of violence against his crews worried Lorenzo. He had already contracted for additional muscle to be shipped to both cities and to McQueen County. The hired guns were already en route. Coming into play in the middle of the Russian attacks was going to escalate the problem, but Lorenzo saw that he had little choice. Cameron wanted it brought under control, and he understood there was no chance of any kind of negotiation. So the import of extra muscle was the only option.

IT WAS LATE when Lorenzo arrived at his apartment building and stepped out of his car in the basement garage. The tail car containing his two bodyguards parked alongside him. Lorenzo climbed out and made for the elevator. He heard the sound of footsteps behind him as he pressed the button to bring the elevator down. That was when he heard the unmistakable sound of suppressed shots. He counted at least six. Behind him a man groaned. Heavy bodies thumped to the concrete. Reaching inside his coat, Lorenzo started to turn. He felt the cold touch of the garrote wire as it circled his neck, pulled tight against his flesh, cutting in so deep his clawing fingers were unable to grasp it. The wire sawed back and forth as the loop sliced even deeper. Lorenzo started to choke. Blood was flowing. A hard knee was jammed against his spine, braced there to increase the pressure....

TONY LORENZO's body was found lying on the dirty concrete in a wide pool of blood. His pair of bodyguards lay close by, both dead from head shots. Their handguns were still in their holsters beneath their coats.

20

"I don't believe this," Kowalski said. "Where did he come from?"

The chase car was coming at them fast, holding the center of the road. Bolan watched it in the rearview mirror as it closed in.

"Maybe the tail car got off a message before they came after us. Cameron sent these guys to deal with the problem."

"What does he think he's going to do? Ram us?"

Bolan shook his head. "No, he wants to get close enough so his partner can get off a good shot."

"This day just gets better and better."

The soldier felt the shock as a bullet hit the rear of the SUV. He couldn't hear the sound of the shot above the roar of the engine, but he knew the shooter was fixing his aim. The rear window blew out as a slug tore through it. Glass fragments were scattered across the interior. More shots followed in a crackling volley of automatic fire

"That's enough," Kowalski yelled in frustration. "I'm not sitting here letting them do all the damn shooting."

She grabbed the SPAS shotgun Bolan had taken from Lonny Magruder. She twisted her body and climbed over the back of her seat, dropping onto the rear cushions. She scrambled over the backrest and braced herself against the side of the rear compartment. She placed the SPAS on the bottom of the glassless frame and fired off two shots from the powerful combat shot-gun. The second peppered the chase car's hood.

"Try for the shooter if he shows himself again," Bolan yelled above the wind noise. "I'll brake."

He saw her nod.

The SPAS angled around as the shooter leaned out through his open window.

"Now," Kowalski yelled.

Bolan touched the brake and the SUV slowed, the gap clos-ing quickly as the chase car failed to draw away fast enough.

The SPAS fired twice in rapid succession, and the chase car's shooter jerked back as his right shoulder took one of Kowalski's shots. His autorifle dropped from his hands. His shoulder had been opened like a side of butchered meat, pulped flesh and shattered bone soaked in blood. The guy slid awkwardly back inside the vehicle.

The chase car held its position as if it was tethered to the rear of the SUV. Kowalski fired again, peppering the hood, and saw the car falter.

"I'm out," she called. "No more shells."

"Brace yourself," Bolan said.

He stood on the brake, feeling the 4x4 shudder, tires burning against the road. The heavy vehicle slid as the wheels locked. Bolan fought to keep the SUV under control. The front wheels hit the loose earth at the side of the road, momentum pushing the vehicle forward. It bounced as it cleared the road and slith-ered around in a half circle, throwing up clouds of dust.

"Get clear," Bolan said, throwing open his door and rolling from the seat. He landed in a semicrouch, the Beretta in his hand as he moved to the rear where Kowalski was dragging herself over the window frame. Bolan caught a handful of her uniform shirt, dragging her free. She hit the ground and rolled to the opposite side of the SUV.

The chase car had jerked to a stop, the driver throwing open his door and exiting in one fluid move. Bolan caught a brief glimpse before the guy was blocked by the rear of the stalled SUV—he was carrying a squat SMG.

Time halted for long seconds.

They were all assessing their next move.

Bolan dropped to a crouch. The chase car driver was at the rear of the SUV. The soldier saw his legs the instant before the guy moved again, this time down the opposite side of the vehicle. He was heading toward the front of the truck.

Damn, Bolan thought. Where the hell was Kowalski?

He saw her as she unwound from her low crouch at the front of the car. Even as Bolan brought her into his field of vision, he saw the man stalking her raise his weapon.

Kowalski had her back to the man, looking in the opposite direction, and Bolan knew he had time for only a single move. He took it, powering out from the vehicle and taking three long strides. His right arm looped around her body as he slammed into her. The deputy gasped as she was propelled forward by the impact. With Bolan's bulk protecting her, she was lifted off the ground and into space. As she fell, the sandy earth absorbing the impact, Kowalski heard the vicious rattle of autofire somewhere behind. Then she was rolling down a shallow slope, drawing breath and spitting out the gritty sand that had passed her lips.

Bolan had rolled clear, the Beretta rising. The shooter was not going to turn and just walk away—he was going to try again.

The Executioner turned onto his back, gun arm extended, and he was already easing back on the trigger when the shooter's outline came into view. The searching muzzle of the SMG showed, too, lining up for a second try. Bolan triggered the Beretta, the triburst finding its target, punching in hard and fast. An instant later two more shots sounded, the slugs slamming into the shooter inches to the side of Bolan's three-round burst. The shooter uttered a stunned grunt as he was flung back by the multiple hits. He landed flat on his back, his body making a final spasm before he became still. Bolan sat up and looked around. Kowalski walked to join him, her service pistol in her hand and an angry scowl on her face.

"What the hell was that all about?" She stared down at the

dead man, then back to Bolan. "I guess I should say thanks. He came out of nowhere. I was sloppy."

Bolan put away the Beretta. "Good hit," he said. "You handle that pistol well."

"I had a good teacher—my dad. I figure it must be in the genes, too."

"You recognize this guy?"

Kowalski took a good look at the man. "He's kind of familiar," she said. "I think I've seen him around town."

Bolan gave a brief nod as he knelt beside the dead man, going through his pockets and transferring anything he found to his own. In addition to the SMG there was a holstered Glock in a shoulder rig beneath the guy's jacket. He held it up for the deputy.

"No amateur," she commented.

"His friends will come looking for him when he doesn't call in." Bolan completed his search and stood up. "It's time we moved," he said.

"I was right when I said I thought I knew him. Jed Tench. I've seen him going in and out of the Cameron Oil office in town, hanging around with Nathan Cameron."

"His hanging days are over," Bolan said.

The Executioner turned as something attracted his attention. He stepped to the rear of the SUV and crouched.

"Gasoline," Bolan said. He stood up. "They blew our tank full of holes. Gas is draining away fast."

Kowalski crossed to the chase car. She stood looking at the hood where her shotgun holes penetrated the metal. When Bolan joined her she gave him a tight smile.

"You thinking what I'm thinking?"

Bolan took a look inside the car. He found the hood release and pulled it so Kowalski could check the damage. His glance took in the shooter Kowalski had caught with the SPAS. He was slumped in the passenger seat, head back. His right arm hung from a few ragged strands of flesh and shredded muscle. Blood soaked his clothing down to his waist where he had bled out. Bolan leaned over and checked for a pulse. There wasn't one.

He heard Kowalski mutter something profane as she inspected the damage. She came around to face him, shaking her head.

"This car is not going home today," she said. "And the only way we are is by walking."

WHEN NATHAN ENTERED the office, he knew he would need to choose his words carefully. Arriving back at the house, one of his men had warned him about his brother's mood. The news about the hit on the weapons convoy dominated everyone's thoughts.

One look at the physical damage only served to caution Nathan even more. Cameron's desktop had been swept clear, sending computer, telephone and everything else across the floor. He had scattered books from the shelves. Nathan quietly closed the door, turning his attention to where his brother stood at the window.

Cameron had an open bottle of whiskey in his left hand. He was taking steady gulps of the liquor. A SIG-Sauer pistol hung from his right hand.

"If Torrance walked through that door this minute, I'd empty this fucking magazine into his skull," Cameron said in a precise, low tone. Nathan realized his brother had already drunk too much—he only spoke like that when he was intoxicated. "Torrance and Magruder. Two armed men. They had the son of a bitch and he still took them down. Then he drove off with Kowalski…" His words trailed off into a heavy silence.

"Lou, I have the boys out looking for Cooper and the girl. I even sent the chopper out. It looks like they headed out into the desert. We'll get them."

Cameron stared across the room at his brother. "That is what I keep getting told, but it's not happening, Nate. Cooper is leaving a trail of dead bodies behind and we are *not getting* him. That mother is laughing at me. Lou fucking Cameron, the Southwest's top arms dealer, who doesn't even have any guns to sell because this guy has just blown my last shipment all over the fucking desert. Jesus, Nate, he's everywhere I turn. Blowing up my organization. Killing my men. And now that goddamn Russian Poliokof is trying to muscle in and take it all away." Cameron gave a choked laugh. "Maybe I should give it all up. Call him and say, hey, Comrade Poliokof, come and get it. I quit. Here it is. My books, my suppliers. Here are the keys to my house and my cars. If I had a fucking cat I'd give you that, too."

Nathan crossed to stand by his brother's side. "No," he said, "we don't even think about that. We don't quit. No way. Yes, this is a crap time for us, Lou, but we'll come through. You built this organization from nothing. You deal all across the U.S. Christ, Lou, all that work, the planning, fighting off the opposition—you want to give it away? Hand it over to those reject Commie bastards? It won't happen. I won't let you quit."

Nathan reached and took the pistol from his brother's unresisting hand. He slid it across the desk after he had ejected the magazine and cleared the cartridge from the breech. Then he gently pried the bottle from Cameron's other hand.

"Lou, you've downed half a bottle. You know how much this stuff costs?"

Cameron made eye contact with his younger brother, a frown creasing his forehead. And then a thin smile cracked his set mouth. He clapped Nathan on the shoulder.

"Very funny, kid," he said.

"Lou, go lie down for a while. Let me take over until you sleep off this very expensive booze. Agreed?"

Cameron nodded and allowed his brother to move him out of the office and through the house to his bedroom. Nathan made sure he was settled, then closed the door and made his way to his own office across the wide hall. He slumped behind his desk, staring into empty space as he went over the recent events.

Two major problems.

The first issue was the activities of Cooper. His campaign against the Cameron organization had, no doubt, caused a severe amount of damage to its reputation. In their business, it was expected that self-protection was a solid and dependable constant. And that had been so until the appearance of Cooper.

Nathan could have ranted and allowed his inner feelings to get the better of him, but yelling and screaming would not alter the facts. Cooper was a formidable adversary. Professional. Ruthless. He favored direct action and did not resort to idle threats. He located his targets and homed in like a heat seeker. He took out property and goods and men with equal intent. His cold efficiency when it came to taking life was one of the most disturbing elements.

It unsettled Nathan. If Cooper came looking for himself and Lou, there would be no negotiating. No pleading for leniency. They were going to need to be on full alert, ready for the man if he came near. The answer was to stop the man before he did come close, deal with him while he was out in the open, being hunted by the teams already on the move.

Nathan understood it wasn't going to be easy. Cooper understood tactics. If his back was to the wall, he would fight hard and any confrontation would be bloody. If that was how it would be, then the sooner the better. They would not be able to start rebuilding the organization until the Cooper had been dealt with.

Nor could they successfully resume the business until Zader Poliokof had been taken care of. Nathan had been doing some discreet checking on the Russian Mob boss. He acknowledged the man's fearsome reputation. Poliokof had risen through the ranks on his own forceful personality, performing so well that his masters back in Russia had offered him a high rank and allowed him to build his own Family. Poliokof had achieved startling success and in the process had engineered the demise of some of his old masters, beating them at their own game.

In a few short years, since moving to America, Poliokof had gathered a fiercely loyal group. They were utterly faithful, in every respect, to Poliokof. No one would even think of going against him because if they did and were caught, their punishment would be too terrible to even contemplate. The savage reprisals against anyone who stood against Poliokof were legend.

His empire prospered, expanded, and it was widely understood that the man wanted more. If he set his sights on something, he invariably got it. One way or another. He would use anything and anyone to advance his interests. Nathan's contacts had told him the word coming from the Russian criminal fraternity was that he had set his sights on the Cameron organization. It had been there for a while, and the destructive maneuvers of Cooper had simply acted as a lit match to the fuse. Poliokof had seized the opportunity to strike while Cameron's problems with Cooper had weakened his hold on his territory. He would keep pushing, taking off sections of the organization and strengthening his intention to snare it all.

Nathan's thoughts were interrupted by the phone. He picked up and recognized the voice as one of the Chicago crew.

"Nate? There's no easy way to say this. Tony Lorenzo was hit a few hours ago. Wire garrote around his neck the same way Costanza was done. Somebody must have been waiting for him when he got to his apartment building. They took him after he got out of his car. Shot both his bodyguards. Lou is going to be pissed. Tony was one of his favorites."

"Keep this to yourself, Artie. I'll tell Lou at the right time. He has enough to deal with at the moment. Lay the word down. I don't want this coming through from anyone. Understand?"

"Okay, Nate." There was a pause. "With Tony gone we don't have…"

"Yeah, I get it. You head things up for the time being, Artie. Poliokof and his crew are a priority. Just let the boys know to watch each other's backs."

"We're on edge here, Nate," Artie said. "Those Russians are coming for us piece-by-piece. We already lost guys here in Chicago and Newark. They hit us hard. Sons of bitches seem to know all our locations."

"Make sure the boys are well-paid for holding out. Help's on the way from Kansas. If these Russians want a fight, they'll get one. Lou isn't going to let this happen, Artie. Stay hard."

Nathan put the phone down. He leaned back in his seat, swinging it back and forth, staring up at the ceiling. The old proverb said something about it always being darkest before the dawn. He tried to imagine how much darker it could get.

He picked up the phone again. Damn thing seemed to be ringing nonstop.

"Yeah? Jesus. Well, tell them that's what they get paid for. To find that bastard and bring him back. Well, if they're on foot that should make it easier. Just do it."

Nathan slammed down the phone. Boneheads. Trouble was they'd had it so easy for so long, now a little pressure was causing them all to whine. What the hell was wrong with them? One guy and one girl, on foot and probably low on ammunition. That's what they were up against—not exactly the Mongol hordes. What did the bastards want? He caught a glimpse of the bottle of whiskey he'd taken from his brother. Nathan got a glass and poured a generous slug. He tasted it, felt it slide down easily.

"If that damn phone rings again before I finish this glass, I'll toss it through the fuckin' window," he said out loud.

The phone did not ring.

Nathan had another drink.

21

They walked for an hour under the hot sun, the wind blowing dust around them in swirls. The sweat produced from their bodies dried on their skin. The single bottle of water from Bolan's SUV had been a third full. They used it to moisten their lips and the insides of their mouths.

"Hell of a hospitable place you have here, Erin."

"You should come around when it's really hot." She moved the M-4 to her other shoulder to lessen the chafing from the strap.

Bolan carried his Uzi in addition to the pair of handguns. They had buried his other weapons and the money satchel some distance from the abandoned SUV. There had been no way they could have dragged the heavy bag along. Kowalski had told Bolan she would be able to locate the ordnance at a later time.

"You still sure you can find that bag again?" Bolan asked her.

She stared at him, then nodded. "Well, I'm pretty sure. They're over that way. Or was it over there? Mmm. Now I'm not so sure 'cause it all looks the same to me."

He realized she was using a slow, dumbed-down accent, deliberately teasing him.

"Okay, Deputy Kowalski," Bolan said, smiling. "I get it. Sorry I asked."

She grinned at him, a playful sparkle in her eyes. "He smiles," she said. "Even in adversity he smiles."

She saw the smile fade. Bolan was looking around, his eyes searching the trackless terrain. Kowalski saw him unconsciously touch the Uzi, fingers gripping the weapon.

"You hear something."

He didn't speak, simply pointed to the west. The deputy spotted the telltale drift of dust. The way it had formed meant only one thing. It was coming from a fast-moving vehicle.

Bolan scanned the area. Behind them a spread of jumbled rocks and boulders formed a wide outcropping. It would at least provide cover.

"Let's go," he said, touching her shoulder to turn her in the direction of the boulders.

As they broke into a run, the tailing vehicle emerged from the dust cloud. Yet another large, roaring SUV.

The sandy ground turned into an uneven stretch of ridged rock. The only thing Bolan could see to their advantage was that the hard surface was easier to run across than drive over.

The SUV was bearing down on them with increasing speed. It cleared the sand and hit the rock layer, wheels bouncing against the uneven surface.

"Go," Bolan yelled.

He caught sight of two passengers in addition to the driver. One in the rear, trying to track in with an SMG.

The SUV tailed them across the uneven strip, bouncing and rocking as the driver kept his foot down hard on the gas.

Bolan and Kowalski had no choice. They ran, their destination straight ahead, hoping they could get to it before the SUV closed in for the kill. At least there would be cover in the outcropping and the pursuing SUV wouldn't be able to negotiate through it.

Behind them the engine rose to a howl as the SUV hit a deep channel and the wheels actually left the ground. When it landed, the engine faltered as the vehicle struggled to regain purchase.

Seizing the opportunity, Bolan stopped, spun, the Desert

Eagle rising in his hand. He tracked in the big handgun and triggered a pair of shots. The boom of the Magnum pistol was loud even in the open space. The powerful .44 slugs went in through the open rear side window, one plowing into the gunner on the seat. The guy uttered a stunned yell as the bullet slammed into his shoulder, ripping its way through muscle and bone. Its trajectory was deflected and it angled deeper into his upper torso, cut through his body and clipped his spine before it blew out and sprayed blood across the interior of the truck. The stricken gunner lost all feeling in his body and flopped helplessly across the seat, then onto the floor.

Two shots were all Bolan got off before the SUV achieved traction again and lurched forward, the driver spinning the wheel as he angled in Bolan's direction.

"Cooper, come on," Kowalski yelled.

Bolan powered away from the approaching vehicle, forcing his aching, weary body to move. He heard the solid beat of the engine coming closer. He ran for his life, knowing that if the SUV got close enough for the front gunner to fire, he would be fully exposed.

He saw a humped ridge in the ground ahead of him and turned to meet it. He didn't break his stride as he jumped the ridge, almost stumbling when he landed on the other side. The screaming howl of the SUV seemed even closer. Bolan pounded forward.

The vehicle hit the ridge, the impact lifting the front end. Then the rear wheels slammed against the ridge and the 4x4 was airborne for a few seconds. As it came down to earth the shock absorbers reacted and the big engine bounced, its own weight and forward motion turning it into an unstable, bulky mass. The driver had lost his grip on the wheel during that moment. He grabbed it back and spun the wheel in a flash of panic. The rocking SUV, already off balance, tried to make a turn against the racked wheel, then flipped over on its side, forward momentum sliding it along the rocky surface.

Hearing the heavy thump, Bolan turned and saw the overturned vehicle caught in a spin that was bringing it even closer to his running figure.

He heard Kowalski yelling.

Heard the squeal of buckling metal.

Bolan took a headlong dive out of the SUV's path. He arched his body, sensing the shadow of the vehicle as he hit the ground on one shoulder, feeling the searing pain that bruised his flesh. Then he tucked and rolled, coming to rest against a low rock. He lay for a moment, dazed and breathless.

"Cooper, they're still moving," Kowalski warned.

Bolan sat up and found he was still clutching the Desert Eagle in his bruised and bloody right hand. He lurched to his feet. Kowalski was coming up from behind, her M-4 A-1 rising as she targeted the front-seat gunner coming up through the passenger door he had shoved open. She hit him with a three-round burst that riddled his upper body. The guy screamed, his chest suddenly bloody. His arm flung skyward, the SMG gripped in his hand flying free. Kowalski fired again, her burst shattering his lower jaw in a burst of bloody gore. The man slid out of sight back inside the vehicle.

Through the shattered windshield Bolan could see the driver fisting a pistol. The guy had pushed himself partway through the windshield opening. He brought his weapon on line, his face contorted with anger, streaked with blood.

"I'll get you, bastard," he screamed.

Bolan two-handed the .44 and punched three fast slugs into the guy. They blew his face apart, cored in through his skull and pasted the back of his head across the angled seat back.

The soldier dropped to his knees, the handgun sagging. The effort of holding it upright seemed too much at that moment. He glanced up as Kowalski appeared in front of him. She knelt, the M-4 A-1 cradled in her arms.

"Cooper, you're a nervy, crazy hombre," she said, her dry throat forcing her words out in a raspy croak. "Still, I'm glad you're on my side."

Bolan managed a lopsided grin. "Me, too," he said.

"Hey, you think there might be something in that vehicle we could use?" Kowalski said. "Like water."

Bolan managed to drag the tailgate open. The rear of the SUV held a cooler bag among the debris that had been tossed around when the vehicle tipped over. Kowalski opened it and they found plastic bottles of water, still on the good side of cool. They stood for a while sipping the water, not gulping it.

"I must look awful," Kowalski commented, running her fingers through her hair.

"Probably not as good as you'd look going out for the evening," Bolan said.

Her uniform was dusty and stained. There was a tear in one sleeve. Dust streaked her hair and face.

"Cooper, are you asking me on a date?"

Bolan raised his water bottle. "Why not, Erin?"

"Hey, I'm not cheap, you know."

"Never crossed my mind."

Bolan raised his head, listening. His acute senses were warning him of approaching danger.

"What is it?" Then her own head turned in the same direction as Bolan's. "Damn. It's a chopper. Coming in fast."

Bolan snatched up the cooler bag and slung it from his shoulder.

"Let's get into those rocks. Go!"

They moved away from the wrecked SUV and cut directly for the spread of rocks. They covered the final couple of hundred yards in quick time. As they scrambled in through the outer ring, the sound of the helicopter rose. Weaving through the scattered rocks, Bolan heard the unmistakable chatter of a machine gun. A ragged line of slugs slapped and tore at the rocks, sending dusty splinters into the air around them. Out the corner of his eye Bolan saw Kowalski stumble, and for a moment he thought she had been hit, but she pulled herself upright and kept on moving. The dark shadow of the chopper overflew them, then it had to bank sharply as the higher ranks of the rocky mass loomed in front of it. Bolan saw it sweep away to the right. He knew it would be back, flying slower to give an observer a better chance of spotting his prey.

"I bet you wish you'd kept one of those rocket launchers behind now," Kowalski said as she followed Bolan into the gap between tall, house-sized boulders.

They rested for a minute. In the near distance they could hear the subdued sound of the chopper as it circled their position. Bolan dropped the cooler bag on the ground and Kowalski took out one of the bottles of water. She took a drink, then splashed some water over her face. It felt good against her dry skin.

"What's our best option travel-wise?" Bolan asked. He helped himself to water.

Once they'd stopped exerting themselves, his abused body let him know its condition. The shoulder he had slammed against the hard ground was aching badly. Bolan massaged it.

"Nothing much around us but more desert. The farther south we go it becomes worse. West is much the same. I think we should head toward the east."

"I'm no tracker," Bolan said, "but doesn't that take us in the direction of…"

Kowalski nodded. "Cameron's place, and beyond that McQueen."

Bolan considered that for a moment. "They might not expect us to do that."

"It could give us the advantage. We come in by the back door and surprise him, so to speak."

Bolan nodded. "We should sleep on it," he said.

"I don't think that's going to happen," Kowalski said.

She saw that Bolan had glanced skyward. His ears had picked up the returning chopper, too. He flattened himself against the gritty boulder, leaning out to get a clearer view. He saw the silver-and-blue helicopter as it dropped to within a few feet of the highest curve of the rocks. It turned sideways, and he saw the hatch had been slid open. Dark shapes moved in the cabin. An armed man stood in the open hatch, then jumped. A second and third man followed.

"Rifle," Bolan snapped and Kowalski handed him the M-4 A-1. The Executioner raised the weapon and triggered a three-round burst that crackled against the chopper's fuselage. He pulled the muzzle toward the front, going for the pilot's cabin. A stream of 5.56 mm slugs starred the Plexiglas, and the pilot reacted swiftly. The chopper banked sharply, pulling away. Bolan raked the underside of the aircraft with the remainder of the magazine. Kowalski had a fresh clip ready and as Bolan ejected the spent one, she passed him the reload. He snapped it in, turning to check where the armed men had jumped from the chopper.

A short burst from an automatic rifle sent slugs into the top of the boulder concealing Bolan. Stone chips filled the air. The soldier pulled back, grabbing the deputy's arm and hauling her to the base of the rocks. She snatched up the cooler bag before he dragged her away from it. Additional autofires, from a second position sent more slugs in their general direction. Bolan led the way deeper into the jumble of rocks.

"What was that remark about sleeping on our problem?" Kowalski asked.

"Yeah, I guess I was a little premature there."

They wormed their way through the narrow gaps between boulders, Kowalski close on Bolan's heels. She had the Uzi slung from her neck, her Magnum revolver in her hand. Within the confines of the rocks, trapped hot air made them sweat heavily. The dust they disturbed as they moved got into their throats, and Kowalski yearned for one of the water bottles she was carrying in the bag slung across her back.

The Executioner put out a warning hand. They halted and he jabbed a hand in the air. Kowalski heard the scrape of boot leather on the rocks overhead. She half turned so she could watch their back trail while Bolan brought the M-4 A-1 into play, the muzzle probing the angles and curves of the bunched boulders. He picked up a slither of sound, then felt the drift of gritty, disturbed dust falling across his shoulders. He pressed back against the face of rock behind him.

Watching.

Listening.

Waiting.

Then he saw the merest shadow as someone moved cautiously. The guy above Bolan tilted his upper body to allow himself the chance to peer down into the gap. From where he half crouched, Bolan saw a head and shoulders edge into view, saw the outline of an SMG. The guy scanned what appeared to be a deserted slipway between boulders—deep shadow forming where the sun was unable to penetrate.

The man convinced himself there was no one beneath him. Just as he was about to draw back he *did* see something—but by the time he acknowledged the fact it was too late.

With his target acquired, Bolan triggered a burst that punched into the guy's upper chest and throat. The 5.56 mm slugs tore at flesh and bone. The man gasped, his only vocal reaction. He jerked upright, lost his footing and slumped on his back. He slid down the curve of the high boulder, into the gap and dropped, slamming to the ground only feet away from Bolan. His weapon followed him.

As the body hit the ground, Kowalski saw an armed figure moving into sight from the direction she and Bolan had come. She brought up her Magnum revolver and hit the moving target as the guy brought his rifle around within the narrow confines of the gap. A pair of 240-grain slugs hit him chest high, knocking him backward. His rifle flipped up as he spasmed, a short burst erupting as his finger jerked the trigger, and he fell to his knees. Kowalski put a third shot into his skull, above his left eye, blowing out the rear of his skull and he was slammed on his back.

"Cooper, you okay?"

"Fine."

Bolan picked up the dropped SMG, hanging it around his neck by the nylon strap. Bending over the dead man, he frisked him and found a backup magazine. He saw that Kowalski had done the same with the guy she had put down.

"We got one more somewhere," Bolan said. "Stay on your toes."

Kowalski holstered her revolver and checked the SMG she had gained.

"I hear that damn helicopter again," she said.

"Touching down. Our one man standing could be getting help."

Bolan gestured to her and led the way deeper into the boulders. If the chopper had landed close to where he and the deputy had entered, then their pursuers were behind and needed to gain ground. Moving farther in gave Bolan and Kowalski extra cover—or so he hoped.

Ahead Bolan saw that the space between the boulders was widening. He cautioned Kowalski to hold back while he checked it out—exposed ground, the rocks diminishing in size, as well.

Kowalski peered over his shoulder.

"Not so good," she said.

"And we still have one guy on higher ground," Bolan reminded her.

Kowalski was silent for a moment. "Cooper, I don't know how you feel, but I'm tired of all this running away. Time *we* did the chasing."

"First thing is to deal with the guy on top." Bolan said.

He made no further comment, turned and moved to where the boulders broke up, exposing the wide, unprotected patch of earth. He gestured for Kowalski to stay close. She stayed on his back, the SMG held tight against her chest. Bolan pointed to the closest available cover.

"Are you crazy?" Kowalski asked. "That's thirty feet of bare ground. He'll see you before you get ten feet."

"Then there'll only be twenty before you bring him down. Make sure that thing is on single shot. Track him, aim and hold, then fire. With luck he'll be standing still. I'm going to be weaving around so he'll need to zero in before he fires. A few seconds, should give you your shot."

"That's a lot of trust you're putting on me."

Bolan simply said, "You can do it."

She checked the SMG again, moving the selector switch, then wiped one sweating hand down the leg of her trousers.

"Let's do this," she said.

Bolan didn't wait any longer. He dug in his heels and took off out of the protective rise of boulders and into the open. Dust puffed up from beneath his boots as he ran.

Kowalski stepped clear, turning to raise her eyes to the slopes of the taller boulders, searching.

Where the hell is he? She wondered.

Bolan was still running, cutting a zigzag trail as he made his move.

Damn, where is the gunner? A moment of sheer panic gripped Kowalski. She couldn't even see…

Finally the guy above rose from his crouch on the high boulder, snapping his weapon to his shoulder, the muzzle moving as he lined up on Bolan's weaving figure.

No chance, Kowalski breathed as she caught the man in her sights, fixing her target and easing back on the trigger. She saw the puff of dust fly from his shirtfront as the slug struck home. His rifle slid away from Bolan. As the gunner struggled to stay on his feet, Kowalski hit him with two more shots, twisting him around. He landed facedown on the surface of the boulder, slowly sliding across the smooth surface.

Bolan skidded to a stop, turned and retraced his way back. He nodded to Kowalski, and they scrambled up onto the lower section of the massive rock, taking themselves to a higher position.

Below, the first group ground-level shooters broke from cover, standing where Bolan and Kowalski had been moments before. They milled about, indecision stalling their movements.

"Go," Bolan said.

He turned and opened up the tight group below.

Three of them. One went down amid a hail of slugs, his body torn by the burst. The other pair pulled back into cover.

Bolan powered up the slope of the rock, catching up with the deputy as she reached the highest elevation. He was about to warn her to stay low when she flattened against the rock, then gestured for *him* to get down.

The chopper stood fifty feet from the base of the boulders. The rotors were turning slowly, idling. The pilot hovered close to the machine, an SMG in his hands.

"You heard that saying between a rock and a hard place?" she asked. "Well, that's us. Only we're on the rock."

Bolan checked the M-4 A-1. "What distance do we have to that guy? Less than three hundred yards?"

"I'd say 225."

"Close enough."

Kowalski watched him shoulder the rifle and sight along the barrel. "Cooper, the minute you fire, those other two are going to come barreling out from those rocks down below."

"You are probably right, so when I drop that guy we head straight down."

Kowalski checked her SMG. "I hope you know what you're doing."

"I do."

Bolan adjusted for angle, took into account the desert breeze and ranged in on the figure below. His finger eased into place, gentle on the trigger and squeezed off his shot. The chopper pilot fell back against the helicopter, then pitched forward on his face.

"Let's do it," he said.

In unison they pushed to their feet and began a headlong run down the curving slopes of the boulders, ignoring the possibility of a fall that would most likely leave them badly injured. There was no grace in the descent. It was, pure and simple, a dash for freedom. Bolan felt a warm spread of moisture as the wound in his side opened and bled. He ignored it. He'd deal with it later.

The Executioner saw ground level coming up fast—faster than he had anticipated—and tried to slow down. That proved to be harder than he had imagined. Off to his left Kowalski was experiencing similar difficulties as she maneuvered across the final twenty or so feet.

Bolan spotted the pair of shooters as they emerged from the ground level access, their weapons coming on-line as they made eye contact. He heard the crackle of autofire and felt slugs bouncing off the surface of the rocks—the shots were wide. The shooters were moving and trying to take out targets on the run.

He jumped the last couple of boulders, saw the ground coming up in a blur. Bolan landed and let his momentum take him forward and down. He hit the ground, spread himself and slid on his stomach, twisting so that he could position himself to face the two shooters as they pulled themselves to a stop.

The crackle of gunfire rattled across the rocks—it was a hectic few seconds. Slugs hit the hard ground close to Bolan as the shooters fired in haste, eager to reach their target. The soldier held only for as long as he could make his shots count. He hit the closest guy with three shots, slugs ripping into the man's right hip, dropping him to the ground in agony. Bolan triggered again and put his next grouping into the guy's chest. The second shooter swung his SMG toward Bolan's prone figure. Before he could pull his trigger, the Uzi in Kowalski's steady hand stitched him across the middle. He fell back with a moan.

Bolan pushed to his feet, aware of Kowalski standing back, watching the guy she had shot. The Executioner put a single slug between the man's eyes, then turned back to her.

"You think they would have cut you a break?"

"I suppose not."

"I've been facing these bastards for a long time," Bolan said. "You'd be facedown in the dirt."

He took her arm and led her to the helicopter.

The deputy composed herself and looked the machine over. "Was it the wisest thing to shoot the pilot, Cooper? Or are you going to tell me you can fly this thing?"

"So maybe I won't. You want to get in?"

Settled in their seats, Bolan ran a check of the controls and instruments, silently thanking David McCarter and Jack

Grimaldi for the time they had devoted getting him trained up to being a reasonably competent pilot.

"I need a drink," Kowalski said, taking a bottle of water from the cooler bag at her feet. She held up the plastic bottle. "And this is all I have when I really need tequila."

Bolan increased the power, feeling the helicopter start to pull against the rotors. He worked the collective, juggling the cyclic stick, his feet on the pedals. The chopper inched off the ground. As he upped the power, feeling the bird responding to his touch, Bolan swung the nose around and watched the ground slip away beneath them.

"Show me Cameron's place," he said.

Kowalski scanned the terrain below, getting a fix, then jabbed her finger in a direction, shouting over the engine noise.

"That way," she said. "Keep your heading and you'll see the house. You can't miss it."

"That large?"

"Oh, yes."

22

An hour later, flying into the coming dusk, Bolan saw the sprawl of buildings that comprised the Cameron property. Lights were starting come on inside the extended house. Floodlights sprang to life, illuminating the wide frontage. Bolan flew in from well behind the rear, slowly descending and aiming the helicopter for the landing pad there.

"Cooper, aren't they going to see us coming? Or is that a stupid question?"

"Yes and no," Bolan said.

He completed the landing with a bone-jarring bump. He shrugged at Kowalski's questioning look.

"Still working on my landing skills."

"I wouldn't have guessed if you hadn't told me."

"They'll be expecting the chopper because it's theirs," Bolan said, "so we'll have a few minutes before they figure out there's something wrong."

"And…?"

"We head for the closest outbuilding," he said, indicating a squat construction off their right. "Cover before they come looking for us."

As the chopper powered down, they made final checks of their ordnance.

"Are you set?"

"This is the day I've been waiting for all my life," she said drily.

"Good. Because I never like to disappoint a lady."

Bolan pushed open the cabin door and dropped to the ground. Kowalski followed suit and they crouched by the front of the chopper. He tapped her on the shoulder and they cut across the flat earth, heading for the outbuilding. They had barely reached cover when a shout was heard.

"Oops," Kowalski said, "I think we're blown."

The rattle of autofire confirmed her statement. Slugs pounded the adobe wall seconds before they rounded the corner. More shots came. Someone was loosing off a great deal of ammunition.

"*Mi casa es su casa* doesn't appear to apply here," the deputy said.

Bolan was looking at their current position in relation to the main house. The light was fading fast, long shadows encroaching on the property. The soldier could hear movement in the vicinity, and he turned as he sensed someone closing in. He spotted an armed figure rising from behind a low wall, brought the M-4 A-1 on-line and hit the guy with a burst. The gunner reared up, weapon slipping from his hands. As that man went down, two more rushed forward to fill the space he had vacated.

Kowalski took her place at Bolan's side, her own SMG adding its sound. They fired in the same moment, catching the pair of gunners with concentrated bursts that dropped them to the ground.

"Over the wall," Bolan said

They cleared the wall, stepping around the downed men, and Bolan led the way through a stone arch that took them into a patio area, with the main house ahead.

"Cooper," Kowalski called.

Her warning preceded the emergence of more armed men coming up on their rear. Bolan heard the deputy yell again and might have continued the fight if her strangled words hadn't alerted him. He turned and saw she had been overwhelmed.

Arms pinned at her side, she struggled to break her captor's grip, despite having a pistol pressed against her head.

"Do it, Cooper. Don't give in to them."

Bolan lowered his M-4 A-1. There was no way he could continue and risk her life. No excuses. He had put them into a bad situation and now Kowalski was under a direct threat.

He raised his hands.

It was not the time to force the issue. That would have to come later.

BOLAN CHECKED his watch. They had been in the cellar of the house for a couple of hours. Their captors had been overly aggressive when they had stripped Bolan and Kowalski of their weapons before dragging them through the house and into the low-ceilinged cellar. A short flight of stone steps led down to the packed earth floor, and the captives were thrown bodily down. The door had been slammed shut and secured, leaving Bolan and Kowalski on the cold floor, bodies aching from the blows and kicks they had received on way.

There was a dull light in the ceiling. It came from a fixture behind thick glass, enabling Bolan to check out the cellar— earth floor, stone walls, no window. The twenty-by-twenty room was bare. No furniture. Nothing stored. Just an empty space.

Bolan had pushed to his feet, stretching his aching bones. One side of his face was raw and scraped, blood oozing from a gash on his lower lip. He crossed to where Kowalski was slowly raising herself. He helped her to her feet, seeing the marks that discolored her face.

"And it was all going so well," she mumbled through bruised lips.

Two hours on they were starting to feel the chill pervading the cellar. Sitting with his back to a wall, Bolan had his arms around Kowalski's shoulders, keeping her close against the cold.

"My dad said that one day all my expectations about romance would hit me in a rush," Kowalski said.

"But not today?"

"Uh-huh. But let's just stay like this for a bit."

DESPITE THE uncomfortable surroundings, Bolan and Kowalski had managed a few hours of sleep. When the door to the cellar was finally opened, Bolan's watch told him it was almost 10:00 a.m.

And Kowalski was no longer by his side. He was alone in the cellar.

Armed men stood framed in the doorway.

"Let's go, Cooper. Sorry you missed breakfast, but it's time to take a ride and go see the boss. He's busy right now, so he wants you in McQueen."

Bolan moved stiffly up the stairs.

"Come on, come on, don't hang back."

Bolan was on the top step.

The man in charge of the team had an impatient expression on his face as he reached to hurry Bolan along.

From somewhere outside the house Bolan heard the sound of autofire—a number of weapons firing.

"What the hell?" the lead guy said.

His attention was drawn from Bolan as he worked on what was happening.

And that was when the Executioner struck.

23

The flight time from Newark to New Mexico had passed smoothly and uneventfully. The private jet belonged to a small company owned by the Russian syndicate, but on the surface it had little connection with Zader Poliokof. Poliokof and his team relaxed—watched a movie, listened to music, talked among themselves. When they touched down someone was waiting for them.

Poliokof was met by a Russian who had his own team with him. Yuri Stetko had worked for Poliokof a long time. They sat in the climate-controlled comfort of the Volkswagen Touareg. There were two more of the powerful SUVs waiting. Stetko was a broad-shouldered man in his early forties, a formidable figure. Below his dark hair, his square face showed his Slavic roots.

"So?" Poliokof asked.

"I used the information you gave me. Cameron is based near a town called McQueen, about a four-hour drive from here. Out of town there is very little—a few ranches, tourist spots. There is also some oil production in the area, and this is how Cameron covers himself. He owns an oil company—Cameron Oil—twenty miles south of McQueen. It does actually produce some product, but it's primarily there to hide his real business. The detail you got from Manny Gottfried led us to all this. Cameron also owns the local sheriff, a man by the name of Torrance, and his chief deputy, Lonny Magruder." Stetko smiled, pleased with himself. "We already picked up Magruder."

"It all sounds very cozy," Poliokof said. "Does Cameron have a big crew around him?"

"He is bringing in outside help, from a man in Kansas named Kassalis. We know about him. He's an independent contractor who supplies outside help for anyone willing to pay. He's sending men to Chicago, Newark and McQueen."

"Cameron is getting worried his own people can't handle things," Poliokof said. "Which is true. His business is falling apart, so he's bringing in help to hold it together."

"It won't do him any good. These American criminals believe they are such hard men. Let them match up against my people—they will fall like dead leaves from trees in winter."

"You have this Magruder you say?"

Stetko smiled. "We picked him up from his home and took him to a safehouse we found way outside town—an old farm that has been deserted for years. We have already gained information from him. It was easy. He squealed like the fat pig he is when we worked on him."

LATER POLIOKOF was able to see for himself how easy it was to extract information from the captive.

Naked and bleeding, his face wet with tears, Lonny Magruder begged and pleaded for his life. In the root cellar of the empty house, Magruder, tied to a rusting metal chair, sobbed unashamedly. The dirt floor under the chair was slick with his spilled blood. His soft face was barely recognizable from the severe beating he had been subjected to, the flesh swollen grotesquely. Stetko's men, well used to this kind of work, had used a number of handy tools they had found in the cellar on Magruder's naked flesh. Torn, mangled strips of flesh hung from his flabby chest and his overweight, pale body sagged in an ungainly posture. The plastic ties pulled tight over his wrists and ankles had already cut off the circulation so that he was unable to pull himself upright again. If it hadn't been for the lengths of electric cable looped around his bulging middle and secured to the chair, the deputy would have fallen to the floor.

"So this is Deputy Magruder. An American cop," Poliokof said, standing directly in front of the mutilated man. "Tell me, Stetko, are we in deep trouble because we have kidnapped this important policeman?"

"Very deep trouble," Stetko said, smirking at the joke. "He has already threatened to have us locked up in jail if we do not free him."

Magruder shook his head violently. Blood and sweat sprayed away from him. "No…I…I…didn't mean that. Please, don't hurt me anymore. I'll give you whatever you want."

Stetko nodded to one of his men standing to one side. The Russian swung the already bloody baseball bat he was holding and brought it down against Magruder's left knee. The force of the blow split flesh and crushed the kneecap. Magruder threw his head back and let out a high shriek of agony. The baseball bat came down a second time, ensuring that the kneecap was beyond repair.

"Ask him what he knows about this man Cooper," Poliokof said.

It took no more persuasion to extract everything Magruder knew about the man.

"On the run from Cameron's men with a female accomplice." Poliokof smiled. "I still want to meet this man. After all, he did kill some of my people in Newark."

"He sounds a little more accomplished than this one," Stetko said, jerking a thumb in Magruder's direction.

"Do you think you have everything he can tell us?"

Stetko nodded. "He told us Cameron uses the office in town as his HQ and keeps all his data there in a computer system. The local police keep watch over the place for him."

"Good. Finish him off. His moaning is becoming a nuisance."

Stetko nodded to the man wielding the baseball bat. He moved in, the bat swinging in a brutal arc as he began to smash it down across Magruder's skull. The sodden sounds of the repeated blows followed Poliokof as he led the way out of the root cellar.

BACK IN THE SUV, cruising steadily in the direction of Cameron's home, Poliokof watched the dry New Mexico landscape slide by.

"I can see why Cameron chose this location for his headquarters—isolated, not heavily populated, and close enough to the border with Mexico so he can both import his weapons and also trade with the drug cartels. They always need weapons. Just like their Anglo cousins. When we take over," he said confidently, "there will be no reason why these conditions should change. You understand the problems the Mexican government has with the drug business, Stetko? We can make money from his situation."

Stetko shrugged as if he did understand but didn't care. All he saw was an open market, with an unceasing demand for quality weapons. The same was almost true as far as the Americans were concerned. Criminal activity in American society was not declining and the groups and the gangs were becoming bolder, demanding better and more guns. To be in control of such an enterprise could mean only one thing. More money. More power. Stetko was not sure which of those appealed more to Zader Poliokof.

The money, or the power?

"Have Cameron's home checked out. Use the information that pig of a deputy gave you. I don't want to put my people into any risky situations. We should know our enemies' home ground clearly before we go in. When we take it, I want Cameron's people dead—all of them. The only exceptions will be Cameron himself and his brother. We keep them alive only until we have what we need from them. I need his contacts, his book, where he keeps his money. Cameron is, after all, a businessman. He will have information I need. After he has given it to me, he and his brother can be disposed of and buried somewhere in the desert. Their final act will be to turn into fertilizer for the plants that grow out there."

24

Bolan turned and elbowed the team leader in the throat. The raw power behind the blow crushed the man's throat beyond any hope of recovery, and he was already on his last breath when Bolan made a successful grab for his SMG and turned it on the assembled group. The closest shooter fell clutching his middle. Beyond him the rest of the group split apart, caught off balance by the sudden change in circumstances. Bolan caught one with a burst of 9 mm slugs that hit the back of his skull, pitching the guy onto his knees. Before he slammed facedown on the floor, the soldier had fired again, this time hitting a pair in the act of unlimbering their handguns. The SMG crackled harshly, blood misting the air as the gunners were blasted apart by the concentrated fire from the weapon. They stumbled and fell, bodies racked with pain, flesh and bone giving in to the hot slugs coring into them. Bolan kept firing, not giving any of Cameron's men a chance.

They were unable to fight back against the furious assault from the man in black. The moment he clicked into this mode, Bolan transformed into a lethal fighting machine. His buildup to this had been rising over the past few days, as he was subjected to the unrelenting violence of Cameron's crew. From Chicago to Newark to McQueen, Bolan had witnessed the morally corrupt empire ruled by the Cameron brothers. The merchandise they traded in, sold into the hands of criminal groups was intended to spread death and suffering to anyone who walked into their path. Illegal weapons, accruing vast amounts of cash, had become Lou Cameron's stock-in-trade. The man had no concerns over the misery caused by the weapons he sold. His long-term ambition was to become the major dealer of stolen weapons, satisfying the needs of his clients. He cared less for the chaos his trade created against the tide of money dropping into his hands. But from the moment the Executioner had dealt himself into the game, Cameron had been given nothing but losing hands.

There was no golden pot at the end of this game.

Only death.

No winner's celebration.

Only the certainty of life being extinguished by the black-clad deliverer of their judgment.

The last man fell, sprawling on the floor in a spreading pool of his own blood, his whimpering cries ignored as Bolan reloaded the SMG with one of the spare magazines taken from the dying and the dead. He jammed others into the pockets of his blacksuit.

Bolan crouched beside the moaning man and turned him on his side, ignoring the protest. In spite of his weakened state the guy was still able to see the former captive's ice-cold eyes.

"Where's the woman? The deputy?"

The guy, sinking into his own pain, simply stared at the grim mask that was Bolan's face. His suffering diminished when he stared into Bolan's eyes.

"The woman," Bolan demanded. "Where is she?"

The man had no will left to defy his tormenter. "Third door along the passage," he whispered, blood streaming from his lips.

Bolan let him go, the man rolling facedown on the blood-slick floor.

As the soldier made to rise, he heard the crash of footsteps—a pair of shooters. Though their weapons were up and ready, they paused as the scene of bloody carnage unfolded before them. In that moment of shock, the pair became unwilling targets as Bolan unleashed the full-auto destruction of his SMG. The weapon spit 9 mm fury, the hot slugs pounding vulnerable flesh and pulverizing internal organs in a few seconds of living horror. The impact of the barrage drove the men back from the doorway, blood spurting, spattering the wall of the passage as they tumbled, jerking and twisting.

Bolan stepped over them, moving along the passage, still echoing to the crackle of gunfire. He strode to the door the dying man had indicated, raising a booted foot to kick it open and following it into the room beyond.

Three men.

One woman.

Deputy Erin Kowalski was tethered to a hard-backed chair, her arms pulled tightly behind her. Her tan uniform shirt had been torn open and half out of her trousers, exposing her upper body. As Bolan stepped into the room, one of the three men was bent over Kowalski in the act of unbuckling her belt, pausing as the shots Bolan had fired broke through his concentration. From the state of his own clothing and the expectant expression on his face it was obvious what would have happened if the man had not been interrupted.

The other two men had already grabbed at the guns left on a nearby table. The Executioner hit them with short bursts that drove them across the floor, screaming in agony. As they fell, he dropped to a crouch, turning the SMG at the third guy, who had thrown himself at the table, one hand extended to snatch up the pistol lying there. Bolan's weapon hosed him with a long blast that tore in through his side, snapping ribs before coring through to internal organs. The guy fell across the table, defying his wounds to grip the pistol. Bolan fired again, the staccato cadence of the weapon accompanied by a rising growl of anger that rose in his throat. The last thing the guy saw was the savage grimace on the Executioner's face before eternal darkness swallowed him.

Among the weapons scattered across the table were a couple of slim, almost surgical-looking knives. Bolan refused to imagine what they might have been used for. He snatched one up, moving quickly behind Kowalski's chair. He severed the cord holding her, then stepped back to replace the spent magazine in his SMG.

"Talk about leaving it to the last moment," Kowalski said. "You practice cutting it fine, Cooper?"

She was talking to cover her distress. As tough as she was, the young woman's true feelings showed through the bravado. Pale-faced, she pulled her shirt together and tucked it back inside her trousers, turned and snatched up one of the pistols from the table. As she stood over the body of the man who had been ready to assault her, she spoke softly.

"Son of a bitch."

"That help?" Bolan asked as he led her to the door.

"I'll think about that and get back to you."

They covered the length of the passage and emerged in the wide entrance area. Bolan pointed them toward the heavy wooden front doors.

"You think we're home alone?" Kowalski asked as they reached the door.

Before Bolan was able to reply, the rattle of more autofire from outside the house reached them.

"I have a feeling we have visitors. And not the welcome kind."

Mere feet from the exit Bolan heard voices. A heavy thud against the door pushed it open, revealing a heavyset man in an expensive suit. Wielding an SMG, he began to lift it in the Executioner's direction.

Bolan powered forward and shouldered the heavy door into the gunner's face. It slammed into the guy, splitting his cheek and pushing him off balance. It gave the soldier enough time to angle his own weapon and trigger a burst into the man's body. The hardman staggered, lost his footing on the top step and toppled backward. He landed hard, his skull cracking against the paving stones.

"Cooper," Kowalski yelled, moving to his side, her pistol targeting the gunners coming around the rear of the big SUV parked near the steps.

Her warning alerted Bolan. He crouched, his SMG coming into play. He triggered a solid burst that hit both men as they cleared the vehicle. One went straight down, and the second fell back against the SUV, a torrent of words bursting from his lips before Bolan fired again. The guy crumpled as the slugs ripped into him, his own weapon spilling from his hands.

Across the far side of the area figures turned at the sound of the shooting. Someone beckoned, and the men started to move in the direction of the house.

"Who are *these* guys?" Kowalski demanded as she and Bolan headed for the SUV. "That wasn't English I heard them speak."

They reached the vehicle and scrambled inside. Bolan tossed his SMG to the deputy. He hit the start button and the SUV burst into life. Dropping the hand brake, he pushed the stick into Drive and stood on the gas pedal. The truck's engine roared as it unleashed its considerable power. Tires squealed on the pavement as it picked up speed, Bolan spinning the wheel to take them away from the advancing group. He heard the distant crackle of autofire, while slugs fell short, kicking up dust. The rear of the SUV slid and Bolan had to work the wheel to regain forward movement. He angled the vehicle toward the open gate entrance.

A gunner rushed out from behind another parked SUV, raising a weapon. Bolan stomped down hard on the pedal. He felt the truck surge forward, picking up speed at a surprising rate. The gunner realized his mistake and tried to jump aside, but he was too slow. The solid front of the SUV hit him dead center. He gave a shrill scream as he was flipped over the hood, rolling up the windshield and across the roof. Turning in her seat, Kowalski saw his body cartwheel off the rear of the vehicle and smash to the ground. He was thrown for yards before his twisted form came to rest.

Bolan took the SUV through the gateway and along the dusty road. Using the comparatively straight run of the road, he kept his foot hard down, leaving the Cameron house far behind.

"That guy you asked about was speaking Russian," Bolan finally said in answer to Kowalski's question.

"You sure?"

"I wouldn't be able to read *War and Peace* in the language it was written," Bolan said, "but I know Russian when I hear it."

She lapsed into silence for a while. Then she said, "Are we talking Poliokof and his Mob here?"

"Yeah."

"All we need next are the triads and we have the full set." She shook her head. "McQueen County used to be reasonably peaceful, Cooper. Then you show up and it's Desert Storm Three."

"You going to arrest me for breach of the peace?"

"Not a bad suggestion, Cooper. At least with you behind bars the war might ease off."

"Unless Cameron and Poliokof are stopped, there won't be any peace. They've brought their poison here. We have to provide the antidote."

The deputy let out a long sigh. "Damn you and your logic, Cooper."

They drove in silence until Bolan asked, "Erin, are you okay about what happened back there?" His tone was concerned, gentle, asking the question but implying no demand for an answer. If she wanted to speak about it, she would on her own terms.

She took her time replying, turning to look at him. "When it was happening I was still so mad for getting myself caught last night. I didn't have time to be scared. Not until that one started to touch my clothes. I saw the look in his eyes. The way he… That was when it started to hit me. And the oddest thought crossed my mind. What would my dad think about it? Would he understand? Craziest thing to worry about. Then you showed up and it all went to hell in a handbasket."

She reached out to touch Bolan's arm. "I never said thanks, Cooper. I won't forget what you did."

"When this is all finished, you can buy me coffee at the diner in McQueen."

"Cooper, you're a cheap date. I'll take you up on that."

Just then something caught Bolan's eye in the rearview mirror. He saw one of the SUVs from the house coming up behind them. It looked to be the same model as the one he was driving, which meant similar power and speed.

"Don't look now," he said, "but our Russian friends are behind us."

Kowalski turned in her seat. "How many more times is this going to happen?" She looked across at Bolan. "This is a normal day for you, I guess."

"I've had quieter ones."

"You realize there's nothing out here liable to help us."

"If these guys came ready for mixing it with Cameron, there could be some extra ordnance in the back. You want to go take a look?"

Kowalski climbed onto the rear seat, leaning over to the luggage area. She was working her way through the carry-alls taking up the luggage space. Finally she said, "My God, these guys are serious. There's enough artillery to take on the National Guard."

"Anything we can use?"

Kowalski appeared peering over the front seat, holding up objects in her hands. "Russian Mob you say?"

"The same."

"But these are not Fabergé Eggs." She let Bolan see what she was holding.

M-67 fragmentation grenades.

Bolan's mind was working quickly. If he could get the pursuit vehicle close enough to drop a grenade inside, it would solve the problem but it would also be tricky to achieve. The Russians weren't going to sit still and let it happen.

"Cooper, he's coming up fast on your side," Kowalski said. "The rear door window is going down. I see a gun."

"Erin, do you have a good throwing arm?"

Her laugh was short. "Hey, two years top pitcher for my high-school baseball team."

"We'll get one chance at this," Bolan said. "I slow down

and you toss that grenade before they realize what we're doing. What do you think?"

"That you just confirmed you *are* crazy, Cooper. It must be catching 'cause I say we go for it."

"Put your window down. Have you had any grenade training?"

"Yeah. They took us through it at the academy. Not that I ever used one since, but I can handle it."

Bolan didn't doubt her word. He checked his side mirror and saw the other SUV swooping in. He held the wheel steady and touched the brake. He wanted to lose speed fast, but not so severe that he caused Kowalski to lose her balance.

"Ready?"

"As I'm ever going to be. Let's do this."

"Now," Bolan yelled and applied more brake.

He saw the other vehicle loom even larger in his mirror as it drew almost level. He saw the reflection of the SMG's barrel jutting from the rear window, expecting the guy to open fire. Then he saw Kowalski's hand and arm swing from her window, saw the dark sphere as she launched the grenade. It cleared the door frame and vanished from sight inside the SUV.

"Go," Kowalski screamed from behind Bolan. He slammed hard down on the gas pedal, felt the SUV surge forward, clearing the other vehicle.

The grenade detonated inside the chase car. There was a split second when silence seemed to cover them. Then the blast reached them in the same moment the SUV exploded, body panels swelling outward, glass fragmenting. The disintegrating vehicle teetered on its front wheels as the rear jumped clear of the ground. It ran off course, swerving away from the road, then became an expanding fireball as fuel ignited. A heavier blast followed—Bolan guessed from more ordnance in the rear.

He brought the SUV to a crawl, turning it around.

"I never thought it would work," Kowalski said. "Cooper, I was looking straight at that guy with the SMG. He was staring back like he couldn't understand what was happening."

"Do the unexpected and it sometimes knocks the other guy off balance for a couple of seconds. That's all it takes."

"Well, we took it this time, Cooper."

"Yes, we did, Deputy Kowalski."

25

When Poliokof walked into the Cameron home, the defenders were either dead or dying. The Russian strode through the wide entrance, polished shoes rapping against the tiled floor.

"Are they here?" he asked.

Stetko shook his head. "Neither of them. We checked thoroughly. No Louis or Nathan Cameron."

Poliokof went to one of the wounded men. He beckoned two of his crew and they hauled the man to his feet. The man had a bullet wound in his left side and was spilling a lot of blood. Poliokof slid his SIG-Sauer pistol from its hip holster and ground the muzzle into the bloody wound. The American screamed loud and long.

"That must hurt," Poliokof said. "Yes?"

The man nodded, his words mumbled as he spoke. "Hurts bad."

"Then I have your attention. We can go one of two ways here. Answer my very simple questions and the pain can be stopped, or refuse to answer I will have your bullet cut out while you watch. Make a fast decision. I don't have all day."

"What do you need?"

"Where are the brothers?"

"I heard Nathan say they were going to check the plant, then go on to McQueen."

"Remember what the deputy told us about the town office," Stetko said.

"His database."

Poliokof raised his SIG-Sauer and fired a single shot into his informant's forehead, taking out the rear of his skull.

"Now the pain has gone. Yuri, any man still alive I want dead, then have this place burned to the ground. Leave a few men to handle that. The rest come with us to McQueen."

THREE SUVs left the Cameron residence. One remained parked outside the house, waiting for the men left behind to search outbuildings and barns. They found stored metal drums of fuel and manhandled them over to the house where they doused the interior. When the SUV drove away a half hour later, flames were already climbing high, fanned by the wind coming in from the outlands.

Dust was starting to blow in from the desert beyond the house. Strong winds gusted in, driving dust into swirling clouds. Visibility dropped. The SUVs drove with their lights on. The GPS units kept the trucks on course. If they hadn't been installed in the vehicles, Poliokof and his crew might never have been able to find McQueen.

MIDAFTERNOON AND THE SKY was darker than normal. Beyond McQueen dust was being drawn up into the currents and fine swirls drifted along the main street. Bolan felt it hiss softly against the side of the SUV. He braked just after the rail tracks.

"Keep going along here," Kowalski said. "The station house is near the far end, just on the cross street."

There was only light traffic. With the storm imminent the inhabitants of the town were heading home.

"You get these storms often?" Bolan asked.

"More likely this time of year, but not too frequently."

They reached the intersection and Bolan made the turn. Ahead and to the left he saw the McQueen County Sheriff's Department. The building stood back from the street and had

its own parking area out front. Bolan counted three vehicles—
two were department cruisers, and one was a plain, unmarked
Ford.

"The civilian vehicle belongs to Eddie Phillips. He works
the communications desk."

Bolan rolled the SUV up alongside the parked vehicles and
cut the power.

"You sure about this, Erin?"

"Yeah. More than I've ever been about anything."

They made their way up the steps and inside the building.
The front desk was deserted. Kowalski pushed through the
double swing doors into the squad room, Bolan close behind.

There was no one in the squad room except for a single, uniformed officer seated at the com center. He was concentrating
on his job so he missed Kowalski and Bolan as they crossed the
room.

"Eddie," Kowalski said quietly.

Phillips turned. He stared at them for a few seconds, giving
no reaction, then let his right hand drop to the butt of his holstered revolver.

"Not the best move you could make," Bolan said, his SMG
leveled at the deputy.

"I'd take his advice, Eddie."

Phillips switched his gaze to Kowalski, shock evident on his
face.

It came as no surprise to either Bolan or Kowalski. They had
to look a sight. Their clothing was streaked and dirty, torn in a
number of places. They both showed bruises and bloody cuts.
Plus Bolan's severe blacksuit made him stand out. They were
both carrying weapons, and the strain of their recent endeavors
showed in their taut expressions.

"What happened to you?" Phillips asked. Then he said,
"Torrance has you two down as armed and dangerous."

"I'll bet the son of a bitch has," Kowalski said.

"Is he in?" Bolan asked.

Phillips made eye contact with the imposing, grim-faced

man. He felt an involuntary shiver when he looked into those ice-blue eyes.

"His office. Erin, what's going on?"

"Where's Lonny?"

Phillips shrugged. "Seems to have dropped out of sight. No one has seen him all day. He kind of vanished."

Heavy footsteps sounded from the far side of the office. Kowalski swiftly crossed it and stood against the wall next to the door that led through.

Walt Torrance walked into the main office, his head down as he studied a sheaf of papers in his hands. He walked right by Kowalski, only looking up when he was in the center of the room. He saw Bolan's blacksuited figure, and the SMG pointing his way. The papers slipped from his fingers and his hand moved toward his revolver.

"Torrance, I wouldn't do that," Bolan said evenly.

The sheriff's face still showed the marks from the last time he had faced Bolan. One eye was blackened and still swollen. His nose and mouth bore livid bruising.

"You're under arrest, mister," he said without much conviction.

"You can quit pretending, Torrance," Kowalski said. She came up behind him and took away his weapon, placing it on one of the desks. She prodded his spine with her pistol. "How about bringing Deputy Phillips up-to-date."

Phillips swung his chair around. "I wish somebody would. Sheriff?"

"He has nothing to say at the moment," Bolan said.

"The hell I—"

"Eddie," Kowalski said, "the sheriff and Lonny have been working for Lou Cameron. Taking his money and providing protection so Cameron could keep his *real* business hidden."

"What business?" Phillips asked.

"Cameron Oil is a front," Bolan said, "that covers Cameron's dealings in illegal arms. He buys and sells high-end weapons. He's one of the top dealers in the country. Weapons he sold were used in a recent shootout in Miami. A number of cops and civilians were killed in that gang-related incident. Cameron had bases in a number of cities. I know because I followed the trail from Miami to Chicago and then Newark. His outfits back there have been badly crippled. I moved here to close down his main base."

"Cooper destroyed a shipment of weapons Cameron was trying to deliver," Kowalski said. "I joined up with him after Torrance and Lonny tried to kill us."

"The bitch is lying," Torrance blurted out.

"No," she said. "I overheard you talking on the phone to Cameron. The day you caught me near your office. You were setting it up to kill Cooper because he was getting onto Cameron's game."

"It didn't work out the way you expected, Sheriff," Bolan said.

"That's why you and Lonny came back all marked up," Phillips said. "You blamed it on a couple of drunks you two had to roust."

"Since Erin and I took out Cameron's convoy, we've been on the run from his men."

"We were held at his ranch," Kowalski said. "But we broke free and ran into another problem."

"Cameron fell out with a crew of Russian Mob up north," Bolan went on. "He didn't handle them right and the guy running it, Zader Poliokof, has his sights set on wiping out Cameron and taking control of the business. He wants to be the man doing all the weapons dealing. They made a hit on Cameron's home just as we broke out."

"Erin?"

"All true, Eddie," Kowalski said. "It looks like we have our own gang war right here in McQueen County."

"Goddamn it, Phillips," Torrance yelled. "They're feeding you bullshit."

Phillips looked from Kowalski, to Bolan and then Torrance. "Somehow I can't believe they just made all that up. You got to admit, Sheriff, it answers a lot of questions. Especially why you and Lonny are so damn friendly with the Cameron boys."

"If we're criminals, Torrance," Kowalski said, "why would we walk back into the department on our own?"

"That's a good point," Phillips said.

"Don't worry too much, Sheriff," Kowalski said. "When we call in the state cops and all, I'm sure things will get straightened out."

"*You…*" Torrance made a sudden, uncoordinated swing at Kowalski, twisting his solid bulk around in a half circle, fists rising.

Kowalski stepped back, away from the move. She held the SMG in her left hand, braced herself and launched a hard right fist that connected with Torrance's unprotected jaw. Bolan saw the blow coming, thought of the deputy's pitcher's arm, and heard the meaty crack as her fist landed. Torrance gave a stunned grunt, his head snapping to the side from the force of the blow. His balance went and he toppled, colliding with one of the desks and falling to the office floor.

Kowalski watched him go down shaking her aching hand, a smile of pure pleasure lighting up her face. "That was a long time coming," she announced, then grimaced as she held up her hand. "Ow, but it hurts, too."

"Deputy Phillips, will you lock him up in one of his own cells?" Bolan asked.

"I surely will," the deputy said.

He took out his pistol and used it to cover Torrance as the man dragged himself upright. Blood was coursing down the sheriff's chin. He stared at Kowalski, his face dark with anger as Phillips led him away.

"It safe to come near you?" Bolan asked.

"I'm cooled down now."

"Better make sure. That was a hell of a right cross," Bolan said, then pointed a finger at her. "I know—your dad taught you that too."

Kowalski slumped into one of the office chairs. She placed the SMG on a desk. "Cooper, I'm whacked out. A wreck. McQueen County is never like this."

"I feel partly to blame."

"Really? Can I get that in writing?"

Phillips came back. "I never knew Torrance had such a catalog of swear words." He looked at Kowalski's hand. "You need some iced water to stop that swelling."

He vanished across the office, and a minute later he returning with a metal bowl filled with water and ice cubes. He placed it on the desk close to Kowalski. She slid her hand into the water, gasping at the cold.

"You guys need coffee?"

Without waiting for an answer he crossed to the office percolator and filled two thick mugs.

"We should let the other guys know," Kowalski said. "Can you call and have them report in?"

Phillips took his seat and got busy at his com unit.

"Will your deputies be okay out in the storm?" Bolan asked.

"Sure. All department patrol vehicles are fitted with GPS. Hard to get lost with those."

Bolan lowered his coffee mug. "That SUV outside could have a tracking device installed. Damn, I should have realized that sooner."

"Does it matter now?" Kowalski asked, not having grasped the meaning behind Bolan's remark.

"It does matter," Phillips said. "It means they can track you right here to McQueen. As far as our front door if they want."

26

The big SUV approached McQueen with the storm still building. Inside the vehicle were the Cameron brothers, a driver and an armed bodyguard riding shotgun. A second crew car followed behind. They were moving relatively slowly due to the dust storm.

The day had turned out to be a disaster for Lou Cameron. It had seemed relatively okay at first. He had Cooper locked up in his cellar, along with the interfering deputy, Kowalski. He had left them there when he decided to make a cleanup visit to the plant, wanting to make certain the facility was secure following the mess with the weapons convoy. When he arrived the entire plant was deserted. Shut down. He found two of his workers dead inside the gate. The rest of the workforce had vanished.

He knew it couldn't have been Cooper. The bodies were still warm, the blood still wet on their clothing. Then Nathan got the call on his cell phone from one of his men at the house—they were under attack.

It had to be Poliokof. The bastard was making his play.

He had ordered his crew to continue onto McQueen. If the house was under siege, it would be suicide to go back.

A little while after they had started for town, one of his men spotted smoke in the distance, coming from the direction of the house.

Confirmation.

Cameron was restless. His mind was closed to everything except what they had come to McQueen for—the information stored on the computer system in the Cameron Oil office. The data, encrypted and hidden within the system, held details of Cameron's suppliers, both military and civilian, home-based and abroad. There were also his financial holdings, and the bank codes of his numerous accounts—all of Lou Cameron's business dealings. He wanted that data. He wanted it now, because the time had come for Cameron, his brother and the men accompanying him to move on.

He had reluctantly accepted that his organization had been brought tumbling to the ground. The responsibility for that rested with Cooper. Neither man had been face-to-face with the other, but Cameron had to live with the fact that Cooper's skill and his destructive qualities had proved to be unbeatable.

He had cleaved his way through the organization from Miami through to Newark, taking out Chicago en route. He had fought off every attempt to stop him, removing Cameron's top men in the process. The nervy son of a bitch, showing a disregard for his personal safety, had taken out a desert convoy and though on the run from Cameron's pursuing crew, had retreated into the desert, then came roaring back for a final showdown.

With the emerging power struggle against Poliokof, Cooper had taken out a team of the Russians in Newark, pitting himself against Cameron's enemies and again had walked away from that encounter. Poliokof's arrogance had even brought him to New Mexico to hit Cameron in his own backyard. It had become clear to Cameron that he needed to back off, move house and establish a foothold elsewhere.

If he stayed here, he could be taken out. With the bulk of his crew being depleted, the time was ripe for a move. He had the finances to establish himself at another location, reconnect with his suppliers and clients and start again. He would do that and defeat his enemies.

"Coming into town, boss," the driver said.

"Stay sharp. Cover the front of the office when I go in. I'll only need a few minutes."

Beside him Nathan leaned forward, staring through the window.

"What if Poliokof's crew is waiting?"

"Hey, bro, take it easy. We'll do this and hit the road."

Cameron tapped the gunner in the passenger seat on the shoulder. "You provide cover when I step out, Harry. But wait until the other car is there to back us. Drivers stay put."

The man called Harry nodded, checking the SMG in his hands.

"Town looks pretty quiet," the driver said. "Storm must have sent everyone home early."

"Just the way we want it," Cameron said.

"COOPER, COME TAKE a look at this," Kowalski said. She was seated at a desk that had a number of monitors mounted in a curved bank. "Video cameras placed around town," she explained. "Watching the bank. Loan office. Traffic control."

"And Cameron Oil," Bolan said, realizing what she was indicating.

"Must be counting the petty cash day," Kowalski said.

Bolan saw two SUVs angled across the street outside the Cameron Oil office. Three armed men stood at the door, and a couple more were in the street, their backs to the office as they stood watch. Each vehicle had a driver sitting behind the wheel, engines idling. Cameron intended to make a short visit to town, prior to leaving.

Bolan crossed to the wall rack that held the department's weapons. He chose a Franchi SPAS shotgun and thumbed eight rounds of 12-gauge shells into the under-barrel tube magazine, then set the weapon for automatic. He picked up Torrance's .44 Magnum Smith & Wesson service revolver, checked the loads and crossed to the rack again. He opened a box of .44 bullets and scooped some into his pocket.

"Cooper?" Kowalski asked.

"You stay here. I'll handle this," Bolan said.

The Executioner walked out of the squad room, out of the building and made his way down to the main street.

As the two drivers spotted him and went for their hardware, Bolan raised the SPAS and put a single shot into the driver's window of each SUV. Glass shattered and the seated figures jerked sideways under the impact of the shotgun's deadly power.

The moment he fired the second shot Bolan moved position, flattening himself against the side of the lead SUV, the shotgun arcing up so he caught the closest gunner as the guy ran to engage. Bolan's dark shape had emerged from the gloom without warning, and he was in position before the guard realized.

The gunner's SMG jutted from the front of the SUV, the guy holding it a couple of seconds behind. He leaned forward to confirm he had seen Bolan and caught the shotgun blast full in the face. The sheer power of the 12-gauge, unleashed from no more than four feet away, took his head apart in a burst of red, leaving a bloody stump behind. Bolan turned and crouch-walked to the rear of the SUV, rounding the vehicle, and emerged on the far side.

The SPAS boomed again, the Executioner firing across the hood of the SUV, catching the second guard between the shoulders. The guy was thrown into the street, his body torn open by the blast. Bolan spun, firing off the remaining four rounds at the men standing by the door of the office. The trio was caught in a storm of 12-gauge shot that shredded flesh and clothing. The blasts became a single sound, the targets twisting and writhing under the onslaught. Blood spurted in glistening streaks, coating the wooden frontage of the building as the ravaged figures went down.

Bolan threw the empty SPAS aside, pulling the .44 Magnum Desert Eagle as he stepped over the bodies and raised a booted foot to kick open the door to Cameron Oil. As it swung inward, the panels shattered, as autofire from inside sprayed the opening. The soldier had already stepped aside, facing the window to the right of the door. He stepped back a few feet, then launched himself at the window, arms raised to protect his face as he burst through the glass, taking the wooden frame with him. He landed on his feet, crouching, and allowed himself to complete a forward roll. He straightened, the pistol in a two-handed grip, tracking the figures clustered around one of the desks.

Lou Cameron, seated at the desk, looked up from the computer he was working at. A section of the office wall had been slid open, exposing a tall, steel-faced cabinet. A man-size door in the panel stood open, and Bolan caught a glimpse of some kind of electronic setup.

Cameron's younger brother, Nathan, was standing at that desk.

To one side was a Cameron bodyguard, wielding a squat SMG, pulling the weapon away from the door to track Bolan.

The Desert Eagle thundered and the gunner was thrown back, as the 240-grain jacketed slug embedded itself in his chest, shattering bones. The guard toppled back and was still falling when Bolan's second shot caught him under the chin and completed the task as it channeled up and blew his brains out through the gaping hole in his skull.

"You got to listen to me. This isn't necessary. We can…" Nathan said, just as he pulled out a pistol from his jacket.

Bolan quickly turned, the Desert Eagle following. It took only one shot to the head, and the man's supposed pleading was ended.

"Goddamn you, Cooper!" Cameron roared. "You killed my brother."

"Just like you killed the father of a four-year-old child in Miami."

"I never ever set foot in Miami," Cameron said. "How could I have killed anyone there?"

"You sold the guns that did."

"No. You can't lay that on me. I sold the merchandise, but I'm not responsible for what the buyer does."

"The denial," Bolan said, the ghost of a smile crossing his face. "Always the denial. You distance yourself from the slaughter created by the weapons you hawk. In Miami five cops and two civilians died. What's the total from all the other victims, Cameron? You work it out. You can count your money easily enough. Try and come up with a human total."

"You wrecked my organization because of a few dead cops? Destroyed my merchandise and killed *my* people, my brother?" Cameron slammed both fists down on the desk, his face suffused with self-righteous anger. "Because of you I got that Russian fuck Poliokof snapping at my heels, killing my crew. He burned my house. He wants my business. Everything. He wants me wrecked. Goddamn you, Cooper, you drew him into this."

"At least we have one thing in common, then," Bolan said. "We both want you dead."

Cameron's rage exploded in a shriek of anguish as he lunged for the pistol lying on the desk. His fingers closed around the checkered grips and he raised it, turning the muzzle toward the grim, black-clad figure standing immobile in front of him.

KOWALSKI, FULLY ARMED, and wearing a protective vest, heard the heavy double crack of the .44 Magnum pistol as she cleared the street and went in through the door of Cameron Oil.

She saw Lou Cameron falling, his upper body punctured by the shots from Bolan's weapon. The head man, and last of the Cameron organization, hit the floor, blood welling up from the fatal wounds in his chest.

"Cooper."

Bolan turned, already replacing the spent cartridges.

"I told you I'd handle this."

"I see that you did. Now think about this. Eddie put out a call to our guys, and told them to watch out for incoming vehicles. One just called in about three SUVs en route for town. Any guesses who it might be?"

"Poliokof."

"It's just you, me and Eddie—the rest of the department is on patrol. They're spread across the county and if we call for them now they aren't getting here in time, except maybe Chris, who called in. So tell me, Cooper, what do we do?"

27

They moved the SUVs, including the one Bolan and Kowalski had driven, to the edge of town and used them to form a roadblock. Kowalski and Phillips dragged the heavy bags holding the Russian weapons out of the rear of the SUV and carried them to a spot well clear of the blockade.

"This *is* going to work?" Kowalski said.

"It's all we've got."

"You know how to cheer a girl up, Cooper."

"It's a talent I have."

"We have grenades here," Phillips called. "Ammunition clips for the guns."

"Load everything you can lay your hands on," Bolan instructed.

He helped himself to a black FN P90. There were several of them in one of the bags. The SMG featured a clear plastic magazine that was mounted on top of the weapon, in parallel formation. The clear magazine allowed the user to make a quick visual check on how many of the fifty 5.7 mm rounds were left. A manual selector allowed semi- or full-auto fire, depending on the extent of trigger pull. Bolan helped himself to a number of extra magazines.

"Poliokof likes to give his boys nice weapons," Kowalski said, helping herself to one of the P90s. "Money's no object, I guess. Who wants to bet that he got them from Cameron?"

Bolan studied the fire zone. His concern was that if Poliokof found his way into town blocked, he might decide to spread his crew and send them around to move from the buildings on either side. He had a feeling the Russian wasn't about to turn around and walk away—not with Cameron's database information waiting for him.

He watched the sky. The wind was still gusting, dust hanging in the air along the street. In another hour it would be completely dark, creating problems for them all.

Kowalski brought him grenades, and Bolan secured them in his blacksuit pockets. She stood beside him as they watched the road beyond town.

Phillips had parked one of the cruisers across the street a couple of hundred yards behind them. He left the lights flashing on the roof to warn off any curious residents.

"This is crazy," he said as he joined them. "This is McQueen, New Mexico, not Chicago."

"You want to go and tell that to the Russian Mob as they make their way here?" Kowalski said.

Phillips adjusted his flak vest. "Not especially." He was loading his own acquired P90, pushing spare magazines and a couple of grenades into his pockets.

"You okay about handling this?" Bolan asked.

Phillips allowed a thin smile to curl his lips. "Don't worry about me, Mr. Cooper, I'll be fine."

THE FOG OF DUST swirling across the open road beyond the town limits cleared as the wind altered course.

Three large SUVs came into view, moving at a steady pace. When the roadblock became apparent, the three vehicles slowed and came to a stop, doors starting to open. Bolan had borrowed a pair of binoculars from the department stores. He raised them and studied the vehicles and the men climbing out. Every man was armed, many of them with the same model P90 Bolan was now carrying. He passed the binoculars to Kowalski.

"He must buy those guns in bulk," she said.

She saw a trio of men climb back into the lead SUV. It

moved off, heading in the direction of the barricade. Kowalski kept her binoculars trained on the vehicle as it closed in. The driver had to have set the cruise control because the SUV kept on coming even as the three passengers jumped clear, opening fire with their SMGs. The heavy vehicle slammed into the center vehicle of the barricade, the weight shifting the SUV enough to open a gap. The three crewmen fired through the gap.

"Cooper, some of them are heading off the road."

Bolan registered what she said. He'd been right. Poliokof was diverting some of his force to circle the barricade and skirt around buildings in order to enter the town.

"Phillips, take the right side," Bolan said. "If you see them, don't try to read them their rights. Just open fire."

Phillips broke away.

"You want me to go over to the left side?" Kowalski asked.

"We don't have much choice," Bolan said. "You watch yourself."

She was gone before he could add anything more.

Bolan had his own problems.

The advance gunners were pushing their way through the gap in the barricade.

The Executioner moved up, well within the two-hundred-yard effective range of the P90. He raised the weapon and fired a short burst that hit the first of the Russians who broke through the gap. The 5.7 mm slugs jerked him halfway around, his suddenly bleeding body jamming the gap, so his partners were forced to physically drag him clear. Bolan had kept moving forward. He could see the other two men attempting to move their fallen buddy. The soldier angled the P90 and let go with a concentrated burst on full-auto, raking the gap and hitting home on the two men. Their screams almost blocked out the sound of the P90's chatter.

Bolan slipped one of the fragmentation grenades from his pocket and pulled the pin. He let the lever pop and lobbed the bomb over the barricade, neatly dropping it on the far side. The detonation rocked the SUVs forming the blockade. He heard frantic yells following the explosion and not one of the voices spoke in English.

He saw a dark figure pushing by the rear of the SUV on his right. The Russian loosed a burst from his subgun, jacking the muzzle left and right before he was fully clear of the vehicle. Bolan tracked in with the P90 and fired off a hard burst that caught the guy's right leg. Blood squirted from the shredded flesh, white bone showing. The man let out a loud howl, his upper body twisting, allowing head and shoulders to expose themselves. Bolan triggered a killing burst that hammered into the guy's skull.

Securing a second grenade, the Executioner ran forward, armed the lethal egg and tossed it in through the shattered rear window of the center vehicle in the barricade. As he withdrew, the grenade blew. It ripped open the SUV and set off the fuel tank under the floor. A hot burst of raw flame engulfed the wrecked vehicle, creating a solid ball of fire that surged up and out. Bolan pulled back even farther as debris rained down across the street.

As the echo of the grenade faded, the soldier heard autofire coming from both sides of the street—from the rear of the buildings Kowalski and Phillips were covering.

BLOTTING OUT THE RATTLE of gunfire, Kowalski skirted the side of Cameron Oil's office and ran down the alley that took her to the back lot. She knew what she would find—cleared ground, a scattering of trash and no appreciable cover.

She flattened against the wall of the building, the P90 held ready. She heard the pounding of running feet, leaned out and saw two gunmen moving in her direction. The deputy picked up on an exchange of sharp conversation. It was not in English. She pushed away from cover, the P90 lining up on the pair. She hit the nearer guy and saw him go down, his body twisting as he struck the hard ground. The second man dropped to a crouch, returning fire, his burst clipping her left shirtsleeve near the shoulder. The burn sharpened her responses. Kowalski stood her ground, angled the SMG and fired on full-auto, her burst catching the guy in the chest. He went over backward, a harsh cry bursting from his lips. He lay kicking frantically, his ravaged body trying to resist the damage done to him by the 5.7 mm slugs. As Kowalski stepped up, kicking his weapon away, he stared up at her, blood bubbling from his lips, and died.

FOR DEPUTY Eddie Phillips it was a return to combat. The deputy, who presented an outwardly reserved personality, had served two tours in Iraq before joining the police. He was a combat soldier and trained in field communications. The post within the McQueen County Sheriff's Department had appealed to him. His two years on the job had been interesting, predictable and had given him insight into rural policing. The events unfolding on this day thrust him back into the world he figured he had left him behind.

He skirted the rear of the print shop standing on the corner of the cross street, cutting his way through empty crates and plastic drums. Ahead a tangle of thick, brush, once cut back but now reemerging, stood as an obstacle in his path. As Phillips ducked low to shrink his profile, he heard the brush ahead of him being disturbed. A man yelled in hard, foreign tones, and a burst of autofire followed the warning. Slugs zipped through the waist-high brush, tearing at the vegetation. They burned the air above Phillips's crouching form. He instantly dropped prone down on the ground. He heard someone crashing through the brush, making no attempt to conceal his passing, as he spit out angry words. Phillips picked out an indistinct shape, the muzzle-flash confirming position as the guy fired again.

"Come to Poppa," the deputy whispered and opened fire, directing his aim at a spot just above the muzzle-flash.

He heard a cry, made out the shadow figure and triggered a second burst that put the guy down hard. The brush crackled again as others milled about in a moment of confusion. Phillips pushed to one knee, fumbled a grenade from his coat, primed it and threw the bomb into the brush. The explosion generated a brief glare and silhouetted yelling men in the millisecond before they were taken apart by the full force of the blast. Phillips stood upright and went into the brush, smoke still curling from the detonation point. Three bodies were crumpled on the blackened ground, one still wriggling in silent agony. Phillips tapped 5.7 mm slugs into the bloody head to end the guy's suffering and moved on.

THE EXECUTIONER saw one of the Russians scramble onto the hood of one of the barricade SUVs. Behind him another gunner was urging him forward. Bolan hit the guy on the hood with a burst from the P90. The man fell sideways, sliding against the windshield, blood streaking the glass. Keeping the trigger back, the soldier targeted the gunner, urging his buddy on, and hammered a half-dozen slugs into the guy's skull. The head blew apart and disgorged a bloody spray as the fatally hit guy dropped out of sight.

Bolan ran to the spot where the Russians had attempted to clear the barricade. He took out a grenade, tugged the pin free and threw the lethal egg to the far side. As the grenade detonated, he flattened against the side of the SUV, ejected the P90's magazine and slipped a fresh one into place. Without missing a beat he vaulted onto the vehicle's hood, spraying the area beyond with 5.7 mm slugs, directing his fire at anything that moved. Two men were down, their bodies shredded and bloody from the grenade. One, two, then three gunners were driven to the bloody ground by Bolan's autofire. The sight of the black-clad Executioner took even the vicious Russian soldiers by surprise.

Adding to their confusion were Kowalski and Phillips as they came angling in from right and left, weapons up and firing, muzzle-flashes cutting through the dusty gloom. The formidable presence of the three Americans overwhelmed the Russian hardmen. They were out of their depth to a degree, men who were more familiar with the urban environment provided by a big city. They gained their reputation via terror and intimidation. Playing on the perception they were unstoppable, they were happier brutalizing a captive tied to a chair.

Nor were they used to the unrelenting onslaught of the man

they knew only as Cooper. His nonstop campaign to bring down Lou Cameron's empire had been more than successful. Zader Poliokof, seduced by the chance to increase his own power and influence, had dragged them into the battle. Poliokof's misreading of the situation had brought him to this life-changing moment.

AS HE SAW his street soldiers fall, their number diminishing, Poliokof understood the concept of defeat and did not like what he saw. His feelings were reinforced when he saw Yuri Stetko on his knees, bloody from head to foot where he had caught much of the blast from one of the fragmentation grenades. His right hand had been blown off, and his upper torso was a ragged and bleeding mass, with rib bones exposed. One side of his face was gone.

Clutching his pistol, Poliokof yelled for his surviving men to fall back to their vehicles. Getting away was the only thing on his mind. He could feel blood running down his cheek from a gash in his head. His expensive clothing was dirty and torn, but right then it didn't matter—only survival mattered.

He reached the rear vehicle of his convoy, fumbling with the door and dragged himself inside. One of his crew was in the driver's seat.

"Get us clear. *Now,*" Poliokof yelled.

The crackle of autofire startled him. Glass imploded from the shattered windshield, shards stinging his face. Poliokof's driver jerked back in his seat, his face removed by the burst from Bolan's SMG.

Poliokof looked out and saw the tall, dark-haired man in the blacksuit, his eyes fixed on the Russian.

Bolan let the P90 hang by its strap as he showed what was in his hands—a pair of fragmentation grenades. With unhurried efficiency he pulled the pins and let the levers spring free. He threw both grenades in through the opening, the spheres dropping between the seats and rolling out of reach.

"I found these in your weapons bag," Bolan said. "Seeing as *you* bought and paid for them, they're all yours."

Then he turned and moved quickly away, leaving Poliokof lunging for the door handle.

Poliokof freed the door and was partway clear when the grenades detonated, tearing the SUV's interior apart. He screamed in agony, his body peppered by steel fragments as the grenade bodies broke apart and the impact of the concentrated blast threw him from the SUV. He landed facedown, his charred and lacerated body writhing. The back of his skull was shattered, and shrapnel had been driven into his brain. His left leg hung by tattered slivers of flesh. He took a few long seconds to die, his final vision of the tall, broad-shouldered man clad in black walking away....

Epilogue

The aftermath took days to clear up. By the time the rest of McQueen County's force returned to town, a great deal had taken place. Deputy Erin Kowalski and Deputy Eddie Phillips had already taken charge. Phillips had made the call to the state capital, requesting assistance with a matter that involved McQueen township having come under attack from rival organized crime figures that included a local figure and elements of the Russian *Mafiya*.

For three days the town was besieged by state police, New Mexico State Highway Patrol and even the FBI. As was expected, the media showed up and there was a frenzy of activity on that front, with wild speculation and some genuine reporting.

Kowalski and Phillips, after hours of grilling by respective superiors, emerged as local heroes—though neither of them sought nor dwelled on that aspect of the matter.

After going through the data residing in Cameron's computer system, the full extent of his business dealings came to light. Sheriff Walt Torrance was down on Cameron's payroll, with records of the money he had been paid to cover Cameron's tracks and look the other way. His guilt was further established when audio recordings of him talking money were found. Cameron, it seemed, liked insurance. The sheriff would end up in prison.

News of the confrontation in McQueen reached the remaining hired guns still on their way. They quietly canceled their journeys and drifted away.

Cameron's Chicago and Newark bases were detailed, as well as countless suppliers, contacts and his myriad bank accounts. The information provided valuable ammunition for the various law-enforcement agencies.

Cameron's empire remained in tatters. His scattered employees, north and south, did their best to remain in the shadows, while some turned on one another, desperate to stay out of the mess by silencing anyone who might incriminate them.

The Russians went underground, maintaining a quiet observance over Poliokof's misdemeanors. For the time being.

The body of Deputy Lonny Magruder was not found until a couple of weeks later. He had been the subject of a statewide Be on the Lookout order once his involvement with Cameron had been established.

The dead located in the desert were all either members of the Cameron organization, or Russian *Mafiya*.

Kowalski and Phillips were keeping mum about Cooper's involvement.

Kowalski and Bolan finally shared the cup of coffee they had promised each other, and the deputy had given the soldier the bag she had retrieved from the desert.

Jack Grimaldi had flown Bolan out of New Mexico the day after the McQueen confrontation. The only complaint he had was the shortness of time he had been able to stay with his lady friend.

Bolan's R & R picked up a few days after he originally slipped away from McQueen, New Mexico. He visited a doctor who liaised with Stony Man. The specialist tended to Bolan's injuries and told him to rest up. The rest lasted for a day before Bolan drove down to Miami and met Gary Loomis for lunch. Loomis didn't push for too many details on what had happened since their last meeting. He had already put together his own scenario and cop or not, he went along with how Bolan had dealt with the matter.

"The information you fed back to me," he said. "It's been a great help, Cooper."

"Glad to hear."

Loomis toyed with his coffee cup. "I still can't figure who or what you really are."

Bolan smiled. "Better it stays that way, Gary."

"Hey, is this one of those I could tell you but then I'd have to kill you things?"

"One thing you can know," Bolan said. "I never hurt my friends."

"None of what you did is going to bring back Jimmy Crockett, or any of those dead cops," Loomis said. "I understand that. But you'll always have support here in Miami. Don't *you* ever forget that."

"How's Emily doing?"

Loomis grinned. "It's going to take time, Cooper, but that little girl will grow up knowing what a hero she had for a dad. We'll watch over her." He fell silent for a moment. "Only thing that pisses me off is knowing that dirtbag Quintain seems to have walked away free and clear."

Bolan didn't say anything to that.

Four days later, Harry Quintain, still living in Miami, but under the constant protection of his bodyguards, was shot and killed by a long-distance sniper while he was on the golf course. As he was in the open at the time, with very little in the way of concealment for a shooter, the shot was considered to have been remarkable. The killing was eventually determined to have been some kind of retribution to do with the Cameron-Poliokof affair.

Gary Loomis knew better.

Bolan knew better.

He was satisfied with the closure. The circle had been completed.